XMAS BREAK

JE ROWNEY

LITTLE FOX
PUBLISHING

Other thriller books by this author

I Can't Sleep
The Woman in the Woods
Other People's Lives
The Book Swap
Gaslight
The House Sitter
The Work Retreat
The Other Passenger
Waking Up In Vegas

Find out more about the author and her books at
http://jerowney.com/about-je-rowney

If you enjoy reading this book, please remember to leave a review. Reviews help readers find new books and help authors to find new readers.

AUTHOR'S NOTE

Xmas Break is a novella, or short novel, set over twenty-five chapters. Should you choose to, you can read one chapter each day in the run up to Christmas. Think of it as your very own thriller advent calendar. As it's a short novel, however, you might prefer to get yourself a mulled wine, hot chocolate or whatever treat you prefer, pull up your blanket, and dive into this festive thriller in one sitting.

Thank you for choosing to read this story.
Wishing you a very happy Christmas,
JE Rowney.

CHAPTER ONE

The scent of vanilla and cinnamon drifted through the living room, a desperate attempt at manufactured holiday cheer from the overpriced candle on the coffee table. Isla pulled her favourite throw blanket tighter, seeking comfort in its soft fleece as she settled deeper into the armchair. The remote felt cold in her hand as she navigated to *It's a Wonderful Life* on Netflix – a Christmas tradition she couldn't quite abandon, even if everything else about the holiday felt wrong this year. December the twenty-third, and she felt anything but festive.

James had bought them a beautiful Douglas fir three days ago. It stood in the corner now, naked except for the lights he'd strung before giving up, waiting for decorations Isla couldn't bring herself to unpack. The bare branches seemed to reach toward her like pleading fingers, reminding her of all the Christmases that had come before. All the Christmases that would never come again.

Three years of silence stretched between her and Clara like a frozen lake – beautiful from a distance, but treacherous to cross. Three years since their mother's funeral, since the inheritance, since everything shattered like a dropped ornament. Isla pushed the thought away, focusing instead on Jimmy Stewart's face on the television screen. She was officially on holiday until New

Year's now. She didn't need to think about the hellish year they'd had.

Just as George Bailey was about to meet his guardian angel, Isla's phone pierced the dim room with its harsh, blue glare. Her heart stuttered when she saw the name in her notifications.

Clara.

Isla's thumb hovered over the delete button, trembling slightly. Clara's name made her stomach lurch, a physical reaction to years of hurt and resentment.

"Isla?" James's voice drifted from the kitchen, followed by the soft pad of his footsteps. "You okay in there?"

She locked the phone quickly, tossing it onto the coffee table as if it had burned her. "Fine," she called back, her voice too brittle to be convincing.

James appeared in the doorway, a steaming mug in each hand. The scent of hot chocolate – her favourite – wafted through the room. His forehead creased with concern as he took in her huddled form on the couch.

"You don't look fine," he said softly, crossing to sit beside her. He handed her a mug, and she wrapped her fingers around it gratefully. "What's going on?"

Isla stared into the swirling foam, watching her distorted reflection. "It's Clara," she finally murmured. "She sent an email."

James stiffened beside her. "Clara? Your sister Clara? The one we haven't heard from since—"

"Since the funeral. Yeah." Isla's voice cracked on the last word, and she took a hasty sip of hot chocolate to cover it. The liquid scalded her tongue, but she welcomed the pain. It was a distraction from the ache in her chest.

"What does she want?" James's tone was carefully neutral, but Isla could hear the underlying tension.

She reached for her phone again, unlocking it with fingers that felt numb. "You're not going to believe this."

James looked at her, willing her to continue.

"She's inviting us for Christmas. To their 'little place in the mountains'," Isla said. The bitterness in her voice surprised even her.

She reached out, retrieved her phone, and opened the message for James to see.

James leaned in, reading over her shoulder. His breath was warm against her cheek. "*We'd love for you to join us*," he read aloud. "*It's been too long, and after everything that's happened...*" He trailed off, looking at Isla. "Well, that's... unexpected."

Isla laughed, a harsh sound that scraped her throat. "That's one word for it."

James came around to sit next to Isla, taking the phone off her to reread the message in full.

"Maybe it's an olive branch?" he suggested, his voice gentle.

"From Clara? Please." Isla stood abruptly, nearly spilling her drink. She paced to the window, staring out at the grey December sky. A few desultory snowflakes drifted past, not quite sticking. "You don't know her like I do, James. Everything's always been a competition with her. Every success, every failure – it's all just ammunition."

"Isla..." James's voice was patient, reasonable. It grated on her nerves. "People can change. This could be her way of trying to make amends."

Isla whirled to face him, her eyes flashing. "Make amends? After what she said at the funeral? After the way she's ignored us for months, knowing what we've been going through?" Her voice rose with each word, emotions she'd been bottling up for weeks finally spilling over.

James stood, crossing to her in two quick strides. He took the mug from her shaking hands, setting it aside before pulling her into a hug. "I know, love. I know."

Isla resisted before collapsing against him, hot tears soaking into his sweater. "I can't do it, James. I can't face her. Not now. Not after..." She couldn't finish, the words sticking in her throat.

James held her tighter, one hand stroking her hair. "Shh, it's okay. You don't have to decide anything right now."

They stood like that for several long moments, Isla's ragged breathing slowly evening out. Finally, she pulled back, wiping her eyes. "I'm sorry. I don't know what came over me."

James cupped her face in his hands, his blue eyes serious. "Don't apologise. Not for this. Never for this."

Isla managed a watery smile, covering his hands with her own. "I..." She paused, thoughts racing. "I can't. I mean. I don't know."

He kissed her forehead, and she smiled, despite everything.

"What would I do without you?" she said.

"What would I do without *you*?" he countered. "Everything you've done for me this year..."

Isla shook her head. "Everything we do, it's for both of us. What would we do without each other?"

"Fortunately, you'll never have to find out. Now, come sit back down. Let's talk about this rationally."

The couple settled on the couch. Isla curled into James's side. He reached for her phone, scrolling through Clara's email again.

"Tell me about this place in the mountains," he said. "Is it a new thing? I thought they lived in..."

Isla nodded. "They do. Or they did last time I spoke to her, but... that was a long time ago."

"I can't believe she's added photos of the place," James said with an almost laugh. "She talks about it like she's an estate agent trying to sell it to you, not your sister inviting you for Christmas break." He waved the screen at Isla. "It's some eco-friendly marvel. All glass and reclaimed wood. Solar panels, geothermal heating. There's even a hot tub on the deck, overlooking the valley."

"Sounds nice," Isla murmured, unconvinced. "But I guess it's exactly Clara's style. Flashy, expensive, and oh-so-environmentally conscious." The bitterness was creeping back into Isla's voice. She took a deep breath, trying to rein it in.

James was quiet, his fingers tracing absent patterns on her arm. When he spoke, his voice was thoughtful. "You know, perhaps this is exactly what we need."

Isla pulled away slightly, looking at him in disbelief. "What?"

"Think about it," he continued, warming to the idea. "We've been in no state to plan Christmas ourselves. Not this year. We've got nothing ready. Not even poor Douglas there. But this..." He gestured at the phone. "This could be perfect. A change of scenery, a chance to get away from..." His gaze swept the cluttered room, lingering on the bare Christmas tree.

"I can't deal with Clara right now," Isla whispered. "I just can't."

"You won't have to, not really," James insisted. "You can take a book, hide in your room. Soak in that hot tub and ignore everyone. Clara will have to understand, after... well, after everything."

Isla bit her lip, considering. The idea of escaping their life for a short time was tempting.

But the thought of facing Clara, of staying in her home, made her want to curl up and hide.

"What if it's awful?" she asked, hating how small her voice sounded.

James smiled, a warm, reassuring smile that reached his eyes. "Then we'll leave. Simple as that. We'll make up an excuse and come home. But what if it's not awful? What if it's actually... good?"

Isla let out a long, shaky breath. She looked around the room. There was nothing festive about it, and for someone who counted down the days to Christmas every other year, that was a stark reminder of how far things had unravelled. This wasn't the holiday she looked forward to anymore — it was the one she feared most: empty and filled with ghosts of everything they'd lost.

"Okay," she said finally, the word feeling strange on her tongue. "Okay, we'll go."

James pulled her close, pressing a kiss to her temple. "It'll be alright," he murmured. "I promise."

Isla nodded against his chest, trying to ignore the knot of anxiety forming in her stomach. She desperately wanted to believe him.

As James reached for his laptop – "We should book our flights now, before we change our minds" – Isla picked up her phone. Her finger hovered over Clara's email, then she tapped out a brief reply:

Thanks for the invitation. James and I would love to come. See you soon.

She hit send before she could second-guess herself, then set the phone down with shaking hands.

"All done?" James asked, looking up from his flight search.

Isla nodded, forcing a smile. "All done."

"It's an hour's drive from the nearest airport. Do you think..." James began. "Would she..."

"I am not sitting in a car with her for an hour," Isla snapped, surprising herself with the sharpness of her tone. She took a deep breath, lowering her voice. "Sorry, I just... I can't."

James raised his hands defensively. "We'll take an Uber," he said calmly.

Isla nodded, grateful that he didn't push the subject. James was good at that—letting her have space to breathe without demanding explanations she wasn't ready to give. She appreciated that, especially now. Clara had a way of twisting words and glances into weapons, digging up old wounds Isla had thought were long healed.

"I'll book the ride once we land," James continued, tapping on the laptop. "Let's make this as painless as possible."

"Thanks," Isla replied quietly. She glanced at her phone. Clara had replied almost immediately. Her message lit up the screen. As though reading Isla's mind, it said:

I'll pick you both up. Don't worry about renting a car. Can't wait to catch up, xx Clara.

The double xx looked so out of place, like an attempt at familiarity where there was none. She could practically feel Clara's forced enthusiasm, trying to make it seem like they were just two close sisters planning a Christmas reunion.

Isla typed out a quick reply: **We'll take an Uber, thanks. See you soon.**

She hit send and set the phone down, her hands still shaking.

James glanced at her. "It'll be fine, you know," he said softly. "If it gets too much, we'll leave early. You don't have to stay a second longer than you want to."

She nodded, knowing he meant well, but a knot of anxiety still tightened in her stomach. She wasn't worried about Clara's words; she could handle those. It was what Clara wasn't saying that bothered her.

As James turned back to his laptop, Isla's gaze drifted to the window. The snow was falling harder now, fat flakes swirling in the twilight. A white Christmas in the mountains. It should be perfect.

So why did Isla feel like she'd just made a terrible mistake?

CHAPTER TWO

The Uber wound its way upwards through the pass, each turn taking them further from civilisation and deeper into Isla's apprehension. Outside, the world had narrowed to an endless procession of snow-laden pines and treacherous hairpin bends. Inside, the silence hung heavy, punctuated only by the rhythmic swish of windshield wipers battling the intensifying snowfall.

Isla pressed her forehead against the cool glass, her breath fogging the window. She traced a small heart in the condensation, then quickly wiped it away. Christmas Eve. The phrase echoed in her mind, bringing with it a flood of memories: the scent of her mother's gingerbread, the sound of carols drifting from the old record player, Clara's laughter as they hung ornaments on the tree...

She squeezed her eyes shut, banishing the thoughts. That was then. This is now.

"It's beautiful, isn't it?" James's voice cut through her brooding. "Like driving through a Christmas card."

Isla tore her gaze from the window, fixing James with a look that could freeze vodka. "Beautiful? It's desolate. I don't understand why Clara would want to live out here."

"You know," James said carefully, "you've never really told me what happened between you and Clara. Why you..."

Isla stiffened, her hands clenching into fists in her lap. "Because I don't want to talk about it."

"But Isla, if we're going to spend Christmas with them..."

"I said I don't want to talk about it." Isla's tone left no room for argument. She could feel James's eyes on her, concern radiating off him in waves.

James sighed, reaching for her hand. She let him take it, but her fingers remained limp in his grasp. His skin was warm against hers, familiar and comforting despite her resistance. "I just think..."

"How much further?" Isla asked the driver, cutting James off. She caught the man's eye in the rearview mirror, noting the weariness etched into his face.

He glanced at them, his eyes wary. "About another thirty minutes, ma'am. If this snow lets up." He paused, then added, "You folks sure about this? It's mighty isolated up there. Especially on Christmas Eve."

Isla nodded tightly, pulling her hand from James's and tucking it under her thigh. "We're sure," she said, even as every instinct screamed at her to ask the driver to turn back.

The car fell silent again, save for the soft Christmas carols playing on the radio. *O Holy Night* drifted through the speakers, the joyful lyrics a stark contrast to the tension in the backseat. Isla hummed along unconsciously, the familiar melody soothing despite her anxiety.

As they climbed higher, the world outside became increasingly monochrome. Snow-covered peaks loomed in the distance, barely distinguishable from the heavy grey sky. Skeletal trees clawed at the clouds, their bare branches weighed down with ice. The road narrowed, becoming little more than a track. Their driver slowed to a crawl, his knuckles white on the steering wheel.

"It's so quiet out here," James murmured, almost to himself. "Perfect for a peaceful Christmas Eve, don't you think? A chance to really connect, away from all the noise and distractions."

Isla didn't respond. Her thoughts were as turbulent as the weather outside.

Christmas Eve. She should be at home, curled up on the couch with a mug of hot chocolate, not hurtling through a frozen wasteland towards a confrontation she'd been avoiding for years. She thought of their apartment, the half-decorated tree, the ornaments still unpacked. The space in their lives that they couldn't bring themselves to talk about.

"Isla?" James's voice was gentle, probing. "Where'd you go just now?"

She shook her head, not trusting herself to speak. James reached out again, this time just resting his hand on her knee. The weight of it was grounding, a reminder that whatever lay ahead, she wasn't facing it alone.

The Uber ride up the mountain had been long and quiet, a heavy silence punctuated only by the occasional crunch of gravel beneath the tyres. Isla's eyes flicked to the passing trees, feeling more and more hemmed in with each bend in the road.

"Nearly there," the driver announced, his voice clipped with relief as if eager to end the journey.

Isla peered through the window just as the trees gave way to reveal a modern house of glass and wood perched on a cliff's edge. The pictures hadn't lied—warm light spilled from the towering windows, illuminating the stark landscape that seemed to swallow the structure whole.

Next to the front door, a neat stack of firewood caught Isla's eye, topped with a gleaming axe that looked more decorative than functional. It was so perfectly arranged it could have been a photo shoot for "Rustic Living" magazine. Isla fought the urge to roll her eyes - of course Clara would manage to make even a woodpile look Instagram-worthy.

"Wow," James murmured, almost to himself. "It's incredible."

Isla grudgingly agreed, but the isolated grandeur of the place only served to heighten her unease. She focused on the thought of being miles away from anyone else, the steep drop beyond the driveway a stark reminder of their isolation.

As the Uber rolled to a stop in the circular drive, she exhaled sharply, already reaching for her wallet. Paying the driver was a small price for avoiding a tense car ride with Clara. The peace, even in strained silence, was worth it.

James got out first, while Isla lingered by the car door, collecting herself. He looked back at her and forced a grin, his eyes searching her face.

"Hey," he said, in that tone he used when trying to calm her. "Let's keep an open mind, okay?"

Isla forced a smile, though it was more like a grimace. "I know."

"Good," he said, and there was a quiet earnestness in his voice. "For both of us. And if it's too much, we can head back early. Promise."

Before she could respond, the front door of the house flew open, and Clara came rushing out, all smiles, dressed in a sleek cream cashmere outfit. Her voice chimed a little too loudly in the stillness.

"You're here! We were starting to worry!"

Clara engulfed Isla in a cloud of expensive perfume and blonde hair.

"Oh, Isla," she murmured, hugging Isla tightly. "I'm so glad you came. This is going to be the best Christmas ever, I just know it."

For a moment, Isla was transported back in time. Clara's embrace felt like home, like childhood Christmases and shared secrets. Then reality reasserted itself, and Isla stiffened, gently extricating herself from her sister's arms.

Over Clara's shoulder, Isla caught sight of Greg hovering in the doorway. Even at this distance, she could see the tension in her brother-in-law's posture, the forced smile on his face. He raised a hand in greeting but made no move to join them in the swirling snow.

Well, Isla thought grimly, *at least I'm not the only one who doesn't want to be here.*

As Clara released her and turned to greet James with equal enthusiasm, Isla took a moment to survey her surroundings. The house towered above them, its windows like watchful eyes. Beyond it, the cliff dropped away into nothingness, an abyss of swirling snow and encroaching darkness.

Isla couldn't shake the feeling that she was standing on the edge of something far more treacherous than a mere overhang. She just hoped she wouldn't fall.

"Come on, let's get you inside," Clara chirped, looping her arm through Isla's. "It's freezing out here, and I've got mulled wine waiting. It is Christmas Eve, after all!"

Clara led Isla towards the house, chattering non-stop about the long drive and the unexpected snow. Isla glanced back at James. He was still by the car, helping the driver unload their bags, ever the gentleman despite the biting wind.

"Go on ahead and get warm," James called to Isla, his voice carrying just enough to reach her. "I'll be right there."

Isla hesitated, watching as the driver handed James the last of their luggage. She couldn't make out what the driver said, but there was a questioning tone in his voice, as if he wasn't quite comfortable leaving them here. James responded with a nod and a quick word that Isla couldn't catch, his back turned towards her.

Isla forced a smile as Clara's voice droned on about the cabin's high ceilings and panoramic views. As the Uber's taillights disappeared into the swirling snow, she had an irrational pang of longing to flag the driver down and tell him to wait—to beg him to take her back to the airport.

Instead, she took a deep breath of the crisp mountain air, trying to centre herself. The cold stung her lungs, sharp and clarifying. It's just a weekend, she reminded herself. You can do this.

And it's Christmas.

It's Christmas.

Making her way towards the house, each step was heavier than the last. The snow crunched under her boots with a sound that seemed oddly final, like something being sealed shut. The house loomed larger as she approached, its enormous windows dark and watchful against the growing gloom.

When Isla reached the front steps, she paused, taking in one last deep breath before forcing a smile onto her face. James caught up with her, and stood by her side, an encouraging look in his eyes, while Clara had already moved ahead, fussing with keys and locks.

Isla exhaled slowly, then climbed the final step, feeling as if she were crossing an invisible line into something she couldn't quite define but knew she couldn't avoid.

CHAPTER THREE

The warmth hit Isla like a wall as they stepped into the building, the sudden change in temperature making her skin tingle. Snowflakes melted on her eyelashes as she blinked, adjusting to the soft, golden light within. Clara's 'little place in the mountains' was even more impressive on the inside – a cathedral of glass and polished wood, with soaring ceilings and a view that stole what was left of Isla's breath.

But it was the Christmas decorations that truly caught her eye. The place looked like it had been torn from the pages of a high-end holiday catalogue. Garlands of pine and holly adorned every surface, their rich scent mingling with cinnamon and clove. Twinkling lights reflected off the glass walls, creating the illusion of infinite stars. A fire crackled in a massive stone fireplace, casting dancing shadows across the room.

"Welcome to our winter wonderland!" Clara exclaimed, spreading her arms wide. Her voice echoed slightly in the cavernous space. "What do you think?"

"It's... something," Isla managed, shrugging off her coat. The wool was damp from the snow, heavy on her shoulders like the weight of her apprehension.

James squeezed her arm as he moved past her, murmuring, "Be nice." His touch lingered a moment too long, as if he was reluctant to let go.

Greg appeared from a side room, his forced smile still firmly in place. He moved with a stiffness that spoke of discomfort, whether physical or emotional, Isla couldn't tell.

"Of course, you remember Greg," Clara said, her tone just a touch too bright.

"Of course," Isla replied, as if it was ridiculous to think she wouldn't. But as she met Greg's eyes, she realised with a jolt that she barely knew this man who had been her brother-in-law for five years. Had his hair always had that touch of grey at the temples?

"Let me take your coats," Greg offered, not quite meeting anyone's eyes. His wavering voice was deeper than Isla remembered, with a rasp that hinted at either too many cigarettes or too little sleep.

As Greg disappeared with their outerwear, Clara led them into the great room. A massive Christmas tree dominated one corner, its branches heavy with ornaments that glittered in the firelight. The tree had to be at least twelve feet tall, nearly brushing the vaulted ceiling.

"Oh!" Clara dipped to pick something off an elegant side table. "Isla, look what I found when I was going through Mum's things."

She turned, holding out a tarnished metal star. Isla's heart clenched. She recognised it immediately – the wonky points, the scratched surface where she'd tried to engrave her name as a child. The memories hit her like a physical blow:

the smell of glue and paint, her mother's warm laugh, the pride that had filled her, seeing her creation atop the tree year after year.

"You made this in third grade, remember? Mum always put it on top of the tree." Clara's voice was full of smiles, but Isla could only remember the jealous child she had been. The sister who had resented Isla's handmade contribution.

Isla nodded, not trusting herself to speak. She remembered making the star, remembered her mother's delight when she presented it. She also remembered the Christmas after the divorce, when their father had sneered at the "ugly thing" and insisted on a store-bought topper instead. The way Clara had stayed silent, neither defending the star nor agreeing with their father.

"I thought we could put it on the tree here," Clara continued, oblivious to Isla's inner turmoil. "A little piece of home, you know?"

Isla forced a smile, feeling it strain at the corners of her mouth. "Sure, Clara. That's... that's nice." The words tasted false on her tongue.

James stepped in, his voice warm. "What a wonderful idea. It's beautiful, Isla. Did you really make that?"

As James and Clara discussed the star, Isla found her gaze drawn to Greg. He stood by the floor-to-ceiling windows, staring out at the swirling snow. There was something in his posture, a tension that seemed at odds with the festive surroundings. His reflection in the glass looked ghostly, superimposed over the stark white landscape beyond.

"Drinks!" Clara suddenly announced, clapping her hands together. The sound echoed off the high ceilings, making Isla flinch. "We need drinks. It's Christmas Eve, after all. I've got mulled wine warming, or there's eggnog, or I could open a bottle of champagne..."

"Mulled wine sounds perfect," Isla said quickly, needing something to occupy her hands and ground her in the present before she drowned in memories.

"James?" Clara turned to him expectantly, a perfect hostess smile plastered on her face.

"Just water for me, thanks," James replied with a polite smile.

Clara's eyebrow arched, a mix of amusement and intrigue crossing her face. "Water? On Christmas Eve? Come now, we must have something more festive for you. How about some sparkling cider? Or I could whip up a virgin mojito?"

James shook his head, his tone light but firm. "Water is fine, really. I could run to a *sparkling* water, if you have one," he smiled. "But don't let me spoil the fun for everyone else."

Isla watched the exchange, a small knot of tension forming in her stomach. She'd almost forgotten that Clara didn't know about James's sobriety. It had been such a part of their life for the past few years that it was strange to see it treated as novel or surprising. He hadn't gone back to the drink, not once, not even when the year had threatened to pull them under. There was tension in her gut, but there was also pride.

"Right, well," Clara rallied quickly, her smile never faltering. "Mulled wine for Isla and me, and a Perrier for James. Greg, darling?"

Greg turned from the window, seeming to come back to himself. "Hm? Oh, wine. Please. Thank you."

He moved to join them, his steps measured, almost cautious.

As Clara bustled off to the kitchen, the click of her heels on the hardwood floors echoing in the sudden quiet, Isla took the opportunity to really look around. The house was undeniably beautiful, a triumph of modern architecture. But there was something... off. The decorations were perfect. Too perfect. It was as if Clara had tried to recreate a Hallmark movie version of Christmas, all shine and no substance.

Isla's gaze fell on a side table laden with framed photos. A familiar pang of jealousy twisted in her gut as she spotted what looked like Clara and Greg beaming in front of the Eiffel Tower. Of course they'd been to Paris. Clara always did have the perfect life. She and James had booked a holiday last year, but things being as they were, it had been cancelled. No refund. No week in the sun. She shook the thought from her mind.

Drawn by a mix of envy and morbid curiosity, Isla moved closer and picked up one of the smooth wooden frames. But as she examined it, confusion replaced her jealousy. The couple in the photo weren't Clara and Greg at all. It was a pair of strangers, smiling at the camera with the iconic tower behind them.

Frowning, Isla set down the picture and picked up another. This one showed the same couple, not Clara and Greg, on a beach somewhere tropical. Her heart raced. She grabbed another frame – the mystery couple again, this time skiing.

"James," Isla called softly, shooting Greg a look before beckoning her husband over. Her brother-in-law had gone back to staring out into the snow, seemingly disinterested in his guests. "Come and see this."

But before James could reach her, the sound of returning footsteps made Isla hastily replace the photo. She turned to see Clara re-entering the room, carrying a tray of drinks.

"Here we are!" Clara's voice was bright, but there was a tightness around her eyes that hadn't been there before. "Who's ready for a toast?"

As Clara distributed the drinks, Isla caught James's questioning look. She gave a small shake of her head, silently promising to fill him in later. The mulled wine steamed gently in elegant glass mugs, the scent of cinnamon and cloves wafting through the air.

"A toast," Clara declared once everyone had a glass. She raised her mug, the firelight catching on her wedding ring. "To family, to Christmas, and to new beginnings."

Isla took a large swallow of her wine, welcoming the burn. As the alcohol hit her system, spreading warmth through her chest, she couldn't shake the feeling that she was missing something important. The house was beautiful, the decorations were perfect, her sister was trying so hard...

But who were the mystery couple?

Isla looked over at her sister, who was handing Greg his wine as though he were a child about to spill it. Clara was three years older than she had been the last time they had seen each other, and still, of course, three years younger than Isla. It was to be expected that Clara had friends that she didn't know. Mr and Mrs Well-Travelled probably had photographs of their best friends Clara and Greg dotted around their home. What did she and James have?

She glanced at Greg, who was staring into his wine as if it held the secrets of the universe. At James, who was examining the room with an interest that seemed just a touch too keen. He loved it, she could tell. For a split second, she wondered if she had made the wrong decision three years ago, but it was another thought she had to shake from her mind. What was done was done.

The metal star, still sitting on the table, caught the firelight, sending fractured reflections across the room. Isla watched the play of light, remembering the little girl who had crafted it with such hope and love.

She felt a million miles away from that child now.

She felt a million miles away from the sister who had once been her entire world and had, over the years, become a stranger.

CHAPTER FOUR

The four drank in silence after the toast. Clara lowered her glass, her eyes shining with what might have been tears.

She turned to face Isla.

"I'm so glad you agreed to come," she said softly. "After everything... well, I wasn't sure you would."

Isla opened her mouth, then closed it again. Mother's voice echoed in her head: *If you can't say anything nice...*

"Isla deserved a break," James cut in smoothly. "We both did."

"Hmm." Clara studied them both over the rim of her glass. "You certainly do. After the year you've both had..."

Isla's fingers tightened around her glass. James's hand found her knee under the table, a gentle pressure meant to calm.

"Let's not get emotional after one mulled wine," Clara said brightly, too brightly. "There's plenty of time for that later." She set her glass down with determined cheerfulness. "How about I show you how the house works instead?"

"Works?" Isla said, and then, "Why not?"

Was this what the holiday was going to be about? Clara showing off, and her trying to pass off her boredom as politeness.

“And now,” Clara announced, her voice brimming with barely contained excitement, “let me show you what makes this place truly special.”

Isla suppressed a sigh as her sister pulled out her smartphone with a flourish. The warmth of the mulled wine was beginning to fade, leaving behind a dull headache and a growing desire to escape to wherever their bedroom was located.

“This little app,” Clara continued, either oblivious to or ignoring Isla’s lack of enthusiasm, “controls the entire house. Watch this!”

With a few taps on her screen, Clara dimmed the lights in the great room. The warm glow faded to a soft twilight, the Christmas tree twinkling even more prominently in the semi-darkness. Another tap, and the tree’s lights pulsed gently, cycling through a rainbow of colours.

“Isn’t it wonderful?” Clara beamed, her face illuminated by the changing hues. “We can control everything from here. The temperature, the blinds, even the music system.”

As if on cue, the opening notes of *White Christmas* played softly from hidden speakers. Isla had to admit, albeit grudgingly, that the effect was impressive. She glanced at James, expecting to share an amused look at Clara’s over-the-top demonstration. Instead, she found him leaning forward, eyes wide, staring at the app with genuine interest.

“This is incredible, Clara,” James said, his voice tinged with awe. “The integration must be complex. How long did it take to set all this up?”

For a split second, Clara’s smile faltered. Isla caught a quick, almost imperceptible glance between Clara and Greg. Then, as swiftly as it had vanished, Clara’s beaming expression returned.

“Oh, it was quite a project,” Clara said, her voice just a touch too breezy. “But it’s worth it. The place is so efficient now. Solar panels, underfloor heating – it’s really state-of-the-art.”

Isla noticed Greg shift uncomfortably, his forced smile barely masking what looked like a mix of embarrassment and unease.

“It’s quite something,” Greg offered, his voice lacking Clara’s enthusiasm. “Shall we show them to their room? Freshen up before dinner.”

His voice sounded detached. There was a forced quality to it that Isla couldn’t put her finger on.

“Of course!” Clara chirped. With another tap on her phone, the lights returned to normal, and the music faded away. “Follow me, you two. We’ve put you in what we like to call *The Pine Room*. I think you’ll love it.”

As they climbed the sweeping staircase, Isla couldn’t help but marvel at the craftsmanship of the house. Every detail, from the hand-carved banister to the artfully placed sprigs of holly, spoke of careful planning and excessive expense.

It was beautiful, undeniably so, but there was something almost aggressive about its perfection.

Clara led them down a hallway lined with generic artwork – landscapes of snowy mountains and frost-covered forests. Isla frowned slightly, surprised by the bland choices. These insipid prints seemed at odds with Clara's usually bold taste. She paused before a door adorned with a delicate wreath of pinecones and ribbon.

"Here we are," she said, pushing the door open with a flourish. "Welcome to your Christmas haven!"

Isla stepped into the room and her breath caught. It was as if she'd walked into a winter fairy tale. Subtle lights were woven through garlands that draped elegantly from the exposed wooden beams. The king-sized bed was piled high with pillows and a thick duvet that looked like freshly fallen snow. A small Christmas tree stood in one corner, decorated with tiny woodland creatures and pinecones.

"Oh, Isla," Clara said, her voice suddenly soft. "Do you remember how you used to love fairy lights as a child? How you said they made everything magical?" She gestured around the room, a hint of vulnerability in her eyes. "I wanted to recreate that magic for you. For both of you."

A lump formed in Isla's throat. The gesture was unexpectedly thoughtful, a glimpse of the sister she'd once been so close to. "It's beautiful, Clara," she managed, surprised by the sincerity in her own voice.

Clara's face lit up, and Isla had a pang of guilt for her earlier cynicism. Perhaps this weekend wouldn't be so bad after all.

"The bathroom's through here," Clara said, moving towards another door. "We've made sure you have everything you could need, but let me know if—oh!"

As Clara opened the bathroom door, Isla let out a startled yelp. There, directly opposite the door, stood a life-sized model of Santa Claus. Its glassy eyes seemed to stare directly at her, its frozen jolly grin more unsettling than cheerful in the confines of the bathroom.

"Oh Isla!" Clara laughed, clapping her hands together. "I knew you'd love it! Isn't it fabulous?"

Isla forced a smile, her heart still racing. "It's... certainly something," she managed.

"Well, we'll leave you to get settled," Clara said, apparently satisfied with Isla's reaction. "Dinner will be in about an hour. Just use the house app if you need anything – I've already set you both up as users."

As soon as the door closed behind Clara, Isla sagged against the wall. "Good grief," she muttered. "I thought I was going to have a heart attack."

James chuckled, pulling her into a hug. "Come on, it's not that bad. A bit kitsch, maybe, but

Clara's clearly tried hard to make this special for you."

Isla pulled away, giving him an incredulous look. "Are you kidding? That thing is creepy as hell, and I'm sure she knew it would freak me out. It might as well be a clown!"

Before James could respond, Isla marched into the bathroom. She tugged off her cardigan and threw it over the Santa's head, obscuring its unnerving stare.

"There," she said, returning to the bedroom. "Much better."

James raised an eyebrow but said nothing. Instead, he began unpacking their suitcases, humming *White Christmas* under his breath.

CHAPTER FIVE

Isla lay on the bed, listening to James cycle through hummed Christmas songs as he unpacked their suitcases. Despite the cosy surroundings and Clara's attempts at thoughtfulness, Isla couldn't shake the feeling of unease that had been growing since they arrived.

"James," she began, her voice barely above a whisper, "something's not right here."

James paused in his unpacking, a neatly folded shirt in his hands. He turned to face her, his brow furrowed with concern. "What do you mean?"

Isla sat up, glancing at the door as if afraid Clara might be listening on the other side. She lowered her voice even further. "The photos downstairs. They're not of Clara and Greg. And did you notice how weird Greg was acting during Clara's little smart home show?"

James sat down next to her on the bed, the mattress dipping slightly under his weight. The scent of pine from the small Christmas tree in the corner mingled with his familiar cologne, a combination that usually comforted Isla but now only added to her sense of disorientation.

"Isla," he began, his voice gentle, "I think you might be reading too much into things. Greg's probably just not as into the tech stuff as Clara is."

Isla studied James's face, noting the slight crease between his brows that always appeared when he was concerned but trying not to show it.

It was an expression she'd seen too often in recent months.

"It's not just that," she insisted, standing up to pace the room. Tiny ornaments on the miniature tree trembled with each of her agitated steps. "This whole place feels... off. Those bland landscape prints in the hallway? That's not Clara's style at all. And the way she kept looking at me, like she was waiting for some specific reaction..."

James watched her, his eyes tracking her movement. He absentmindedly fiddled with the edge of the duvet, a habit Isla recognised from countless late-night conversations. "Look," he said finally, "I know this isn't easy for you. Being here, trying to reconnect with Clara after everything that's happened. It's bound to be a bit strange."

Isla stopped pacing, turning to face him. The room was suddenly too small, too festive, like a Christmas card come to life but with sinister undertones. "You think I'm imagining things."

"No, not imagining," James said carefully, standing up to join her. He placed his hands on her shoulders, his touch warm through the thin fabric of her sweater. "Just... maybe interpreting them through the lens of your history with Clara. It's been a long day, we're both tired from the journey. Why don't we get ready for dinner? Things might seem clearer after we've eaten."

Isla wanted to argue further, but the gentle rationality in James's voice made her pause. His thumbs traced soothing circles on her shoulders, a gesture so familiar it almost broke through her anxiety. Almost.

"Fine," she sighed, stepping back from his embrace. "But I'm keeping my eyes open."

James smiled, but it didn't quite reach his eyes. "That's my girl. Always the detective." His tone was light, but something in his expression seemed off. Before Isla could analyse it further, he'd turned away, back to their suitcases.

As James busied himself with their clothes, Isla found herself drawn to the window. Outside, the snow was falling harder, thick flakes swirling in the glow of strategically placed outdoor lights. The effect was beautiful, like being inside a snow globe. But it also emphasised how isolated they were up here, cut off from the world.

"I'm going to grab a quick shower," James announced, interrupting her thoughts as he hung his last shirt. He paused at the bathroom door, that same odd expression stuttering across his face. "Try to relax, okay? It's Christmas Eve. We should be enjoying ourselves."

As the shower started, Isla laid out her dress for dinner – an appropriately festive deep green velvet number. The fabric caught the glow from the fairy lights, shimmering like pine needles in the winter sun.

She ran her hand over the soft material, trying to summon some enthusiasm for the evening ahead. But her mind kept circling.

The sound of the shower shutting off snapped her back to reality.

"All yours," James said cheerfully as he emerged from the bathroom, a cloud of steam following him. He was wearing a towel wrapped around his waist, his skin still damp. "I left the, uh, jolly fellow covered up. Though I swear his eyes follow you even through the cardigan."

Isla managed a weak smile. "My hero," she said, grabbing her toiletry bag and slipping past him into the bathroom. The mirror was fogged up, and Isla imagined she saw words written in the condensation. But as she blinked, it was just her own reflection staring back, wide-eyed and uncertain.

Under the hot spray of the shower, Isla's thoughts drifted to the past few months. The long days, the whispered conversations in institutional corridors, and finally, the quiet grief that had settled over their home. It had been exhausting, both physically and emotionally.

This getaway, strange as it was, could be exactly what they needed. A chance to step away from the lingering sadness that had permeated their lives. Perhaps a week in the mountains, surrounded by the trappings of Christmas, could help them remember how to smile again.

By the time she'd finished getting ready, Isla had made a decision. She would try to embrace this vacation, to give Clara and her over-the-top

Christmas enthusiasm a chance. James was right; they deserved a break from their everyday reality.

"Ready?" James asked as she emerged from the bathroom. He looked handsome in a dark suit, a sprig of holly pinned to his lapel. The deep green of the leaves matched Isla's dress perfectly, as if they'd planned it.

Isla nodded, smoothing down her dress. "As ready as I'll ever be," she replied, reaching for her favourite pair of earrings - delicate silver snowflakes, a gift from James on their first Christmas together. They reminded her of happier times, before recent events had cast their shadow over their lives.

As she fastened the earrings, Isla's hand moved to her neck, fingers tracing the empty space where her necklace should be. She turned to James, who was adjusting his tie in the mirror.

"James," she said softly, "could you help me with my necklace?"

She held out a slender silver chain with a small, elegant pendant. It was simple compared to the opulent decorations downstairs, but to Isla, it was priceless - the only piece of jewellery she owned that had once belonged to her mother. Everything else had gone to Clara.

James took the necklace, his fingers brushing against her palm. "Of course," he murmured, moving to stand behind her.

Isla lifted her hair, exposing the nape of her neck. She watched in the mirror as James carefully draped the chain around her throat, his slim fingers working the delicate clasp.

As the pendant settled against her skin, James's hands lingered on her shoulders. Their eyes met in the mirror.

"Isla," James said carefully, "are you wearing this as a message to Clara?"

Isla's hand flew to the pendant, her fingers curling around it protectively. "I... I'm not sure," she admitted. "Maybe? Is that terrible of me?"

James turned her gently to face him, his hands warm on her arms. "No, not terrible. Just... are you sure you want to stir things up tonight?"

Isla sighed, leaning into his touch. "I don't know, James. Part of me wants to pretend everything's fine, to just get through this week without any drama. But another part..."

"Wants to confront the past?" James finished for her.

She nodded, feeling a lump form in her throat. "Is that wrong? To want to... I don't know, to make her see..."

James pulled her into a tight embrace, cutting off her words. "It's not wrong," he murmured into her hair. "It's complicated. But maybe... maybe we should take this one step at a time. Get through dinner first, see how things go. Okay?"

Isla took a deep breath, inhaling the familiar scent of James's cologne. "Okay," she whispered. "You're right. One step at a time."

They stayed like that, drawing strength from each other's presence. Finally, James pulled back slightly, cupping Isla's face in his hands.

"Hey," he said softly, "no matter what happens down there, remember - we've got each other. That's all that matters."

Isla managed a small smile, covering one of his hands with her own. "You're right. Thank you, James. For everything."

James leaned in, pressing a gentle kiss to her forehead. "Always, Isla. We're in this together."

With a final squeeze of her hand, James moved to sit on the edge of the bed. Isla joined him, smoothing her dress as she sat. They were ready to face whatever the evening might bring, but for now, they savoured this moment of quiet togetherness.

CHAPTER SIX

Isla looked over to the window, gazing at the snow-covered landscape outside. The fairy lights strung around the room cast a warm, golden glow, their gentle twinkle reflecting in the glass. She turned her eyes to the small Christmas tree in the corner.

"It really is beautiful," she murmured, more to herself than to James.

"The view?" he asked.

"The tree. Look at it, James," Isla said. "The ornaments, the lights... Clara's put more effort into this guest room tree than I could muster for our entire house this year."

James's eyes followed hers to the meticulously decorated tree. "It is impressive," he agreed. Then, with a hint of amusement in his voice, he added, "Though who puts Christmas trees in guest bedrooms?"

Isla chuckled softly. "Clara does, apparently."

They sat in companionable silence, taking in the festive scene. Finally, James spoke. "Should we head down, do you think? Or wait to be summoned?"

Isla bit her lip, considering. The thought of facing Clara and Greg sent a fresh wave of anxiety through her. "We... we could wait a few more minutes," she suggested hesitantly. "Just us?"

James smiled. "I think that's a great idea."

They sat side by side on the edge of the mattress, their shoulders touching. James's arm found its way around Isla's waist, the familiar weight of it comforting, an anchor in the sea of uncertainty in which she was drifting.

"You look beautiful, by the way," James said softly, his eyes meeting hers.

Warmth bloomed in her chest, chasing away some of the chill that had settled there since their arrival. She leaned into James, resting her head on his shoulder.

"Thank you," she whispered. "For everything. For being here, for encouraging me to come... for just being you."

"I know this is tough for you," James murmured, his breath warm against her ear. "I'm so proud of you for coming. For trying."

Isla turned to face him, studying the lines of concern etched around his eyes. When had those appeared? She reached up, tracing the curve of his cheek with her fingertips.

"I'm grateful for your support," she said, her voice barely above a whisper. "I couldn't do this without you."

James caught her hand, pressing a kiss to her palm. "Hey, none of that. You've supported me through everything. I'm always here for you, Isla. Always."

He paused, a wry smile tugging at the corners of his mouth.

"We might not have as much as Clara and Greg, but we have each other. That's worth more than any smart home gadget or designer outfit."

"You're right," she said, allowing herself a small chuckle. "And honestly, I'm not sure Clara and Greg have as much as they want us to think they do."

James raised an eyebrow, encouraging her to continue.

"Did you notice how... detached Greg seemed?" Isla continued, lowering her voice instinctively. "When Clara was showing off all the smart home features, he looked like he'd rather be anywhere else."

James nodded slowly. "Now that you mention it, yeah. And Clara... I don't know. Something about her enthusiasm seemed a bit forced. Like she was trying too hard to impress us."

Isla sat up straighter, turning to face James fully. "Exactly! It's like they're putting on a show. Remember how they used to be? Always finishing each other's sentences, laughing at inside jokes?"

"And now they barely look at each other," James added, his brow furrowed in thought. "I caught Greg staring out the window earlier, looking... I don't know, lost? Trapped?"

Isla nodded eagerly, grateful that James had noticed it, too. "Clara keeps touching him - his arm, his shoulder - but it seems more like she's staking a claim than showing affection. And did you see how he tensed up every time?"

"I did," James said, his voice low and serious. "You don't think... I mean, they seem to have it all, but do you think they're having problems?"

Isla bit her lip, considering. "I wouldn't be surprised. All this..." she gestured around the room, "it feels like overcompensation. Like Clara's trying to paper over the cracks with luxury and perfection."

James was quiet, his hand absently rubbing circles on Isla's back. "You know," he said finally, "seeing them like this... it makes me even more grateful for what we have."

A lump formed in her throat. "What do you mean?"

"Us, Isla," James said, his eyes meeting hers with an intensity that took her breath away. "We might not have the fanciest house or the latest gadgets, but we have trust. We have honesty. When things get tough, we face them together."

Tears pricked at the corners of her eyes. "We do, don't we? Even when..."

"Even then," James said firmly, knowing without words what she was referring to. "Especially then. That's what real love is, Isla. It's not about the good times. It's about holding each other up when things fall apart."

Isla leaned in, pressing her forehead against James's. "I love you," she whispered. "So much."

"I love you too," James replied, his voice rough with emotion. "More than anything. We're going to get through this week, and whatever comes after. Together."

Isla had a renewed sense of determination. Whatever games Clara was playing, whatever was going on between her and Greg, it didn't matter. She and James had each other, and that was enough.

A sharp rap at the door shattered the moment.

Isla and James froze, exchanging wide-eyed glances. Had whoever was at the door heard their whispered criticisms? Heat rushed to her cheeks, her heart suddenly pounding.

James squeezed her hand reassuringly before standing to answer the door. Isla held her breath, straining to hear.

The door creaked open, revealing Greg's imposing figure silhouetted in the hallway. His face was impassive, betraying no hint of whether he'd overheard their conversation.

"Dinner's about to be served," Greg announced, his voice flat and emotionless. "Clara asked me to fetch you."

James nodded, his posture relaxing slightly. "Thanks, Greg. We'll be right down."

Greg gave a curt nod and turned on his heel, disappearing down the hallway without another word.

James closed the door, leaning against it with a sigh of relief. "Well, that was..."

"Awkward?" Isla supplied, standing to join him. "Tense? Mildly terrifying?"

James chuckled, pulling her into a quick embrace. "All of the above. Ready to face the music?"

Isla took a deep breath, inhaling the comforting scent of James's cologne one more time. "As ready as I'll ever be."

They made their way out of the room, James's hand a steady presence on the small of Isla's back. The hallway seemed longer somehow, the generic landscape prints watching their progress with judging eyes.

As they descended the stairs, the scent of roast goose and mulled wine wafted up to meet them. The great room below was a symphony of Christmas cheer - twinkling lights, soft carols playing from hidden speakers, and the warm glow of the fireplace all working together to complete the vibe.

Greg was waiting for them at the bottom of the stairs, still as a statue.

"This way," he said, gesturing towards the dining room.

Isla's heels clicked against the hardwood floors, the sound unnaturally loud in the tense silence. James's hand found hers, their fingers intertwining. She squeezed gratefully, drawing strength from his touch.

As they entered the dining room, Isla couldn't help but gasp. The table was a masterpiece of

Christmas excess. A snow-white tablecloth provided the canvas for an elaborate centrepiece of pine boughs, holly, and glittering ornaments. Candlelight danced off the polished silver and fine china, creating an almost ethereal glow.

Clara materialised from the kitchen, resplendent in a crimson dress that seemed to shimmer in the firelight.

"There you are!" she exclaimed, her voice pitched just a touch too high. "I was beginning to think you'd got lost."

Isla forced a smile, acutely aware of James's steadying presence beside her. As Clara enthusiastically began to describe the menu, Isla caught James's eye. He gave her a small, encouraging smile, a silent reminder of their earlier conversation. *We have each other*, his eyes seemed to say.

CHAPTER SEVEN

Greg stood behind his chair, his earlier nervousness now masked by an oddly formal demeanour. Was it Isla's imagination, or did his smile seem a fraction too fixed? Had he heard their whispered observations about his marriage?

"Your timing is perfect," Clara smiled, seemingly ignoring the fact that she had sent her husband up to fetch them. "I was just lighting the last candles."

Isla felt James's hand at the small of her back, gently urging her forward. The gesture was familiar, comforting, but something about Greg's careful positioning as they passed – not quite meeting their eyes – made her skin prickle.

"Isn't it beautiful?" Clara trilled, gesturing to the dining table with the flourish of a game show host revealing a grand prize. "Isla, you're here, next to James. I know it's not the traditional way, but I'm going to sit across from you here, and James, you'll be..."

"Right here," James said, nodding at the remaining place.

The elaborate table settings, each marked with a hand-calligraphed name card nestled in a tiny sleigh. Pinecones, dusted with what appeared to be actual gold paint, were artfully scattered between crystal wine glasses and multiple sets of silverware. The overall effect was less festive dinner party and more luxury department store window display.

The massive dining table stretched out before them, its extra place settings conspicuously absent. In their place, shadows pooled in the empty spaces where family should have been - spaces that seemed to whisper of Christmases past, of their mother's laughter, of all they'd lost. The intimacy Clara had clearly aimed for with just the four place settings instead highlighted the absences, making the table feel more like a stage set than a family gathering.

"You really didn't have to go to all this trouble," Isla managed, fighting the urge to roll her eyes at the excess.

"Oh, nonsense!" Clara beamed, adjusting a napkin that was already folded into a perfect Christmas tree shape. "It's Christmas Eve! And we so rarely get to host family."

The word 'family' hung in the air like frost, delicate and sharp. James guided her into her designated seat with a smile. The chair – pulled out by Clara with another flourish – was decorated with a velvet bow that matched the runner on the table.

"Greg, darling, the champagne?" Clara's voice carried a hint of steel beneath its sugar-coating.

Greg moved to the bar cart like an automaton, his movements stiff and mechanical. The crystal glasses caught the candlelight, sending prisms dancing across the stark white tablecloth.

With Isla and James seated, the hostess with the mostest went about her duties.

"I'll just fetch the appetisers," Clara announced, her heels clicking a sharp rhythm as she disappeared into the kitchen.

The champagne bottle trembled in Greg's hands as he reached for James's glass.

"No, Greg—" Clara called from her route to the kitchen, but it was too late. The golden liquid was already cascading into the crystal.

James cleared his throat softly. "Actually, I..."

Greg's face drained of colour. "Oh no. Oh no, I'm so stupid. You said —" The bottle clinked against the glass as his hand shook. "I'm such an idiot. So stupid. Why can't I remember anything?" His voice dropped to a mutter, the self-recrimination seeming excessive for such a minor mistake.

"It's really not a problem," James said, but Greg was already backing away from the table, still muttering to himself.

"Water," Greg mumbled. "Fetch water."

Isla shot James a look, barely concealing her amusement. When he looked back at her with a more serious expression than she had expected, she pursed her lips. There was something going on with Greg, but perhaps it was something beyond his control, a condition he was dealing with and bearing without sharing the details of with his wife's estranged family.

Silently, Isla resolved to be kinder.

Clara returned bearing four bowls of soup with the practised grace of a woman who had studied Martha Stewart videos. Her smile remained fixed in place, her lipstick a perfect crimson slash across her face. She saw Greg teetering and shook her head, smile unwavering.

"I'll get you some sparkling water, James. Greg, darling, why don't you sit down?"

Clara returned with James's water, the crystal decanter catching and fracturing the light from the numerous candles she'd placed around the room.

"Now then," she said brightly, "shall we start with the soup?"

Isla's spoon froze halfway to her mouth as the familiar aroma hit her. Butternut squash, nutmeg, and... something else. Something that transported her instantly back to their mother's kitchen, to Sunday afternoons with flour on their noses and hope in their hearts.

"Is this..." she started, her voice catching.

"Mum's special recipe," Clara finished, her eyes gleaming. "Do you remember the secret ingredient, Isla?"

The words came unbidden to her lips. "Two kisses... one for each of us."

It had been their mother's way of seasoning the soup – two quick dashes of sherry, one for each daughter, accompanied by an exaggerated "mwah!" that never failed to make them giggle. It had seemed magical then, the way those two little "kisses" transformed the soup into something extraordinary.

Now the memory stung like she'd pricked her finger on the holly centrepiece, sharp and unexpected.

"Those Sunday cooking lessons," Clara continued. "Remember how Mum would tie our aprons so tight we could hardly breathe?"

Greg's spoon clattered against his bowl, the sound unnaturally loud in the enormous dining room. He mumbled an apology, his hands visibly shaking as he reached for his water glass, nearly knocking over one of Clara's perfectly positioned candles.

"How's work going, James?" Clara pivoted smoothly, her tone determinedly cheerful. "Still with the same firm?"

"Yes, though there have been some changes recently..." James launched into a careful description of his company's restructuring, while Isla pushed her soup around the bowl, no longer hungry. The golden liquid swirled like memories she'd rather forget.

The conversation limped along, punctuated by long silences and awkward attempts at reconnection. Clara mentioned a movie she'd seen recently; Greg stared at his soup. Nobody mentioned the past, or why they were really there.

Finally, Clara stood, smoothing her crimson dress. "Time for the main course, I think. Greg?"

Greg jumped slightly at his name. “Yes, of course. The dishes...”

He reached across the table to pick up Isla and James’s bowls, stacking them without removing the spoons. Carrying theirs in one hand and his and Clara’s in the other, he followed his wife.

They disappeared into the kitchen, leaving a wake of tension behind them.

Isla turned to James, tears pricking at her eyes. “We shouldn’t have come,” she whispered. “This is—”

A crash from the kitchen cut her off. The sound of breaking china was followed by Clara’s voice, too low to make out the words but sharp with impatience. Greg’s response was equally muffled, but clearly distressed.

James reached for Isla’s hand under the table, beneath the perfectly pressed napkin that now lay crumpled in her lap. Before either of them could speak, Clara’s voice rang out with forced brightness: “Everything’s fine! Just a little accident!”

Isla’s fingers tightened around James’s.

The two empty chairs across from them looked suddenly ominous. How long would Clara and Greg be in the kitchen? What were they really discussing in those urgent, angry hushed tones?

More whispers drifted from the kitchen, punctuated by cabinet doors opening and closing with increasing force. Isla strained to make out the words, but could only catch fragments: "...can't keep..." and "...not now, not tonight..."

"Should we check on them?" Isla whispered to James, but he shook his head slightly.

"Give them a moment," he murmured, his thumb tracing circles on her palm under the table. The gesture, usually comforting, now felt like they were conspirators in something they didn't quite understand.

The Christmas tree lights reflected in the windows, turning them into dark mirrors. Isla caught glimpses of their own faces, pale and uncertain in the glass, overlaid against the swirling snow outside. The effect made them look like ghosts at their own dinner party.

Another crash from the kitchen, smaller this time, followed by what sounded suspiciously like a sob. Clara's voice rose briefly: "Just once, Greg. Just one perfect night..."

Isla's free hand found the edge of the tablecloth, fingers working the expensive fabric. The elaborate place settings now seemed almost grotesque in their perfection – the gold-painted pinecones like little weapons, the holly centrepiece's thorns catching the candlelight like tiny knives.

"James," she started, but before she could continue, the kitchen door swung open.

Clara emerged carrying a massive silver serving platter, her smile firmly back in place, though her lipstick was slightly smudged at one corner. Greg followed with a gravy boat, his earlier trembling now a full-body tension that threatened to spill over at any moment.

"Sorry for the delay," Clara chirped, her voice an octave too high. "You know what they say about too many cooks!"

But as she set the platter down, Isla noticed something that made her blood run cold. Clara's perfectly manicured hands, always so steady, were shaking just as badly as Greg's.

They brought out vegetables, potatoes, the makings of a lavish Christmas Eve dinner, but Isla could think about was how quickly this perfect Christmas façade was crumbling. Like the frost patterns forming on the windows, beautiful but ultimately fragile, destined to shatter at the slightest touch.

CHAPTER EIGHT

Clara set the silver dome aside with another theatrical flourish. "Ta-da! Christmas goose with all the trimmings!"

Steam rose from the perfectly browned bird, carrying the scent of sage and citrus. Around it, roast potatoes glistened like amber jewels, and bright cranberries nestled among sprigs of rosemary. The whole tableau looked like something from a Victorian Christmas card.

"Greg will do the honours, won't you, darling?" Clara's voice held that edge again, the one that made Isla's skin prickle.

Greg nodded jerkily, rising from his chair. He retrieved an electric carving knife from a side table, the cord trailing behind him like a nervous snake. His hands trembled as he plugged it in, and Isla noticed a fine sheen of sweat on his forehead despite the perfect ambient temperature of the room.

"I always say there's something so *traditional* about carving at the table," Clara continued, rearranging the cranberries with precise movements. "Though Mother always insisted it should be done with a proper carving knife. But times change, don't they?"

Greg positioned himself, the electric knife hovering over the goose. When he pressed the button, the mechanical whirr seemed unnaturally loud in the vast dining room. The blade vibrated in his unsteady grip.

James leaned close to Isla's ear, his breath warm against her skin. "Here's Greggy," he whispered, mimicking Jack Nicholson's infamous *Johnny* line with disturbing accuracy.

Isla shot him a sharp look, but a snort of laughter escaped before she could stop it. She quickly raised her napkin to her face, shoulders shaking with suppressed giggles. Trust James to find gallows humour in the situation.

Clara's eyes darted between them, her smile tightening. "Something amusing?"

"Just excited for the goose," James covered smoothly. "It looks magnificent, Clara."

The electric knife buzzed angrily as Greg made his first cut, the blade skittering slightly off course. Isla watched in horrified fascination as he sawed through the bird's flesh, his movements becoming increasingly erratic. Each slice was slightly askew, creating a zigzag pattern that would have given any chef nightmares.

"Careful, darling," Clara murmured, her knuckles white around her wine glass.

The overhead chandelier cast Greg's face in harsh shadows, highlighting the tic in his jaw and the way his eyes darted around the room like a trapped animal's. Outside, the wind had picked up, sending ice crystals tapping against the windows like impatient fingers.

"The goose really does look wonderful, Clara," Isla offered, trying to smooth over the moment.

She accepted a plate of precariously sliced meat, doing her best to ignore how the pieces resembled a jigsaw puzzle someone had assembled in the dark.

"Thank you." Clara beamed, though the smile didn't quite reach her eyes. "I found the recipe in one of Mother's old cookbooks. Remember how she used to say that Christmas dinner wasn't Christmas dinner without a proper goose?"

Greg's hand jerked slightly as he served James, sending a few pieces of meat sliding dangerously close to the edge of the plate.

"Would anyone like more wine?" Clara asked, already reaching for the bottle. "Oh, not you, of course, James. Sorry. Again."

James smiled amiably.

"It's not a problem," he said. "I would love some of those sprouts though, please."

Clara practically glowed as she passed the serving bowl across the table. "Of course. Take as many as you like. There's plenty extra if we need them."

The dish was already filled with more of the perfectly round vegetables than they could manage to eat between four. In addition, there were further dishes that Clara had manifested to the table containing glazed carrots, parsnips and the greenest peas that Isla had ever seen.

They loaded their plates, and an uncomfortable silence fell, broken only by the gentle clink of cutlery against china. Isla took a bite of goose, which was surprisingly tender despite its haphazard presentation. Through the dining room windows, she could see the snow falling more heavily now, the flakes catching the light from the chandelier.

"So, James," Clara said, her voice bright with forced cheerfulness, "you usually spend Christmas with your family? It must be strange being away from them this year."

Isla's hand tightened around her fork. Under the table, James's knee pressed against hers – a silent signal of support.

"Not really," James replied, his voice carefully neutral. "The past few months have been... complicated."

Greg suddenly became very interested in his roast potatoes, pushing them around his plate with methodical precision.

"Oh, of course," Clara said quickly. "I didn't mean to... that is, I know with your aunt's..." She trailed off, flushing.

"These sprouts are delicious," Isla interjected, desperate to fill the awkward silence. "Is that chestnut I can taste?"

"Yes!" Clara seized on the topic with obvious relief. "And pancetta. Though Mother always said—"

James's napkin slipped from his lap and he reached to the floor to retrieve it, his hand skimming Isla's calf as he brought it back up.

She smiled, a flush of red rushing to her cheeks.

The overhead chandelier flickered once, so briefly that Isla thought she'd imagined it. She glanced up, fork halfway to her mouth. The fairy lights seemed to pulse, like a response to the chandelier's uncertainty.

"Did anyone else—" she began.

The chandelier flickered again, longer this time. The Christmas tree lights stuttered in sympathy, their programmed sequence faltering. Even the instrumental carols playing through hidden speakers wavered, a single wrong note stretching into discord.

"Oh, don't worry," Clara said quickly, reaching for her phone. "Sometimes the power gets a little—"

Everything stopped.

The darkness was instant and absolute. Every light, from the soaring Christmas tree to the tiny fairy lights woven through the garlands, died simultaneously. The music cut out mid-carol, leaving a silence so complete that Isla could hear her own sharp intake of breath.

Only the candles in the dining room remained. In the distance, from the great room, the fire maintained its steady glow.

"Clara?" Greg's voice held a note of panic. "What's happening?"

“Don’t worry,” Clara said quickly, fumbling with her phone. “It’s just a power cut. The backup systems should...” She stopped, staring at her dark screen. “That’s strange. The app isn’t responding.”

Outside, the wind had picked up, howling around the corners of the house like a living thing. The sound seemed louder now, without the buffer of ambient music and general electronic hum they hadn’t even realised was there.

“I’m sure it’s just the storm,” Clara continued, her voice tight with forced brightness. But Isla could see her sister’s hands shaking as she repeatedly jabbed at her useless phone.

Nobody moved. They sat frozen around the table, watching the candle flames dance, casting their glow across the half-eaten meal. The goose’s carcass looked particularly macabre in the uncertain light.

The perfect smart house had gone dark, and with it, any illusion of control to which Clara had been clinging.

Isla stared into her half-empty wineglass, watching the candlelight ripple across the dark liquid. Just a storm, she told herself. Just a regular power cut. It happened all the time in bad weather, didn’t it? Even to state-of-the-art smart houses on remote mountainsides.

Remote mountainsides. Goodness, what had they been thinking?

"We should probably check the fuse box," James suggested, his voice steady despite the tension Isla could feel in his grip.

"No need," Clara said quickly. Too quickly. "The house has automated systems for everything. I'm sure it will sort itself out in a minute."

Automated systems. Of course. Because Clara's perfect house wouldn't have anything as mundane as a regular fuse box that actual humans could access. Isla fought the urge to laugh hysterically. They'd driven up a mountain in the dead of winter to spend Christmas with her estranged sister in a house that was too smart to need human intervention. What could possibly go wrong?

The wind rattled the windows, making the candle flames dance wildly. In the shifting light, Clara's crimson dress looked almost black, like a spreading stain across the pristine tablecloth.

"Well," Clara announced brightly, "we can't let a little power cut spoil our Christmas Eve dinner. The goose will get cold." She lifted her fork with determined cheerfulness. "Besides, candlelight is more festive anyway, don't you think?"

The flames made the carved meat look less like dinner and more like evidence. Isla forced herself to take a bite. The goose was still warm, but somehow it had lost its flavour, as if the darkness had stolen its taste along with the light.

"The potatoes are excellent," James offered into the strained silence.

"Thank you," Clara beamed, though her smile looked more like a grimace in the low light. "I used Mother's recipe. Though I could never quite get them as crispy as she did. A dusting of flour and the hottest goose fat. Do you remember, Isla? How she'd always save the crispiest ones for us?"

Isla nodded mechanically, pushing a potato around her plate. Every childhood memory Clara brought up was more like a weapon now, aimed straight at her heart.

Greg hadn't touched his food since the lights went out. He sat rigid in his chair, staring at something beyond the candlelight that only he could see.

"Greg, darling," Clara's voice had an edge to it. "Your dinner's getting cold."

Greg started, as if waking from a trance. "Yes, of course. Sorry." He picked up his fork, his hand trembling so badly that the metal clinked against his plate.

The wind howled outside, and somewhere in the house, something creaked. Isla told herself it was just the building settling, but in the darkness, every sound seemed loaded with meaning.

"More wine?" Clara reached for the bottle, but her usually precise movements were jerky, uncertain. The neck of the bottle clinked against Greg's glass, a sharp sound that made everyone jump.

"Sorry, sorry," Clara muttered, more to herself than anyone else. "It's just so dark, isn't it? But it's fine. Everything's fine."

Isla caught James's eye. His face looked drawn, worried. She tried to smile reassuringly, but suspected it came out more like a grimace.

They continued their meal in near silence, broken only by the scrape of cutlery against china and the constant moan of the wind. Each bite was an endurance test, a performance of normalcy while the darkness pressed in around them.

"I suppose dessert will have to wait," Clara said finally, her attempt at lightness falling flat in the heavy air. "Until the power comes back, of course. Which should be any minute now."

But the darkness showed no sign of lifting, and as they sat, surrounded by the remnants of their interrupted feast, Isla couldn't shake the feeling that this was just the beginning.

The perfect Christmas dinner, like everything else in Clara's perfect house, had crumbled into shadow.

CHAPTER NINE

A sharp sound pierced the tension. Clara's phone's shrill ring cut through the darkness like a knife. In the dim light, Isla saw Greg's hand jerk, sending his fork clattering against his plate. The sound echoed in the vast dining room, competing with the wind's hollow moan outside.

Clara fumbled in her pocket, her dress rustling like dead leaves. She glanced at the screen, and something like panic flashed across her features. The crystal angel hanging on the Christmas tree behind her caught the candlelight, casting a wavering halo around her head that made her look almost spectral.

"Oh! I should... I need to take this." She grabbed one of the candles, nearly knocking it over in her haste. Wax splattered onto the pristine tablecloth like droplets of blood. "Just... just some work thing. Won't be a moment."

"Work?" Isla frowned, watching the dark stain spread across the white linen. "On Christmas Eve?"

"You know how it is." Clara's laugh sounded brittle, like stepping on thin ice. "Some people have no respect for holidays." She was already backing toward the kitchen. The nutcracker statue in the corner seemed to turn its head to watch her go. "Greg, darling, entertain our guests, won't you?"

Greg's head snapped up like a puppet on a string. "Yes, of course. I... yes."

As Clara disappeared into the kitchen, her hurried whispers barely audible, an awkward silence descended on the dining room. Greg cleared his throat several times, his fingers drumming an erratic pattern on the tablecloth. The sound reminded Isla of rainfall, or perhaps tiny footsteps.

James, seemingly unaffected by the mounting tension, continued eating with mechanical precision. The scrape of his knife against the fine china made Isla's teeth ache. How could he eat at a time like this? But then again, James had always been practical. *Keep your strength up*, she could almost hear him thinking.

"So," Greg said finally, his voice oddly high-pitched. "Do you... do you like mountains?"

Isla exchanged a quick glance with James, who paused mid-chew. "Mountains?"

"Yes, mountains. They're very... tall." Greg laughed, a strange, choking sound. "And snowy. Like this one. The mountain we're on. Right now." He picked up his wineglass with trembling fingers, almost missing his mouth as he took a gulp.

From the kitchen, Clara's voice rose briefly: "No, no, everything's fine. We just need a little time to—" Her tone slipped back to an urgent whisper.

"The snow is quite something," James offered, spearing another piece of goose with deliberate care. The meat glistened in the candlelight.

"Snow!" Greg seized on the word like a drowning man grabbing a rope. "Yes, snow. White. Very white. Did you know there are different kinds of snow? The Inuit have fifty words for—" He stopped abruptly, his face contorting. "Though that's actually a myth. About the fifty words. I read that somewhere. Or maybe I didn't. I don't... I can't remember."

Isla pushed her plate away, her appetite completely gone. The vegetables, artfully arranged just a quarter of an hour ago, now looked like they were decomposing in the twinkling light. The cranberry sauce had congealed into dark pools that reminded her of something best not thought about at dinner.

More fragments drifted from the kitchen: "If you could just wait until morning... Yes, I understand it's your—" The rest was lost in a particularly strong gust of wind that set the chandelier crystals tinkling like distant, joyless bells.

"Windy. In here." Greg sounded as though he was talking to himself, rather than to his guests.

"Greg," Isla said carefully, watching his face. "Are you feeling alright?"

"Alright? Yes, fine. Perfectly fine. Why wouldn't I be fine? Everything's fine." His laughter had an edge of hysteria now. "Just sitting here. In the dark. With snow. On a mountain. In our house. Our lovely house that we definitely—"

"Greg!" Clara's sharp voice cut him off. She stood in the kitchen doorway. The perfect hostess mask had slipped, revealing something desperate underneath. "I mean... I need your help with something, darling."

Greg practically leapt from his chair, knocking it backward. The sound of the legs scraping against the polished wooden floor made Isla flinch. Greg hurried into the kitchen without a backward glance, nearly tripping over his own feet in his haste.

Isla could hear Clara and Greg's urgent whispers now, though she couldn't make out the words. She leaned closer to James, who was still steadily working his way through his meal.

"Something's wrong," she breathed.

James nodded slightly, his hand finding hers under the table. His palm was cool and steady against her clammy fingers.

"With Greg?" he said. "Sure is. What's going on with that guy?"

"With both of them. With the house. Tonight. Everything."

James shrugged and took back his hand to continue eating.

Isla screwed up her eyes and shook her head. "How can you...?"

"I'm hungry," he said. "And this goose is..." He stuffed another forkful into his mouth, chewed, and swallowed before finishing his sentence. "...amazing."

"James!" Isla was almost breathless. "We should never have come here. Those two couldn't be any freaking weirder if they tried. I know Clara and I have had our differences, but this is just too much. All the memories she keeps dragging up." Isla visibly shuddered to prove her point.

"Perhaps she's had time to think. You know, since..." James waved a hand and refilled his fork.

"And inviting us here to gloat over her perfect little mountain getaway is... what? Her way of making things right with me? After she cut me off. After..."

The candle flickered, casting an orange glow over James's face.

He paused, the fork midway between plate and mouth, and looked at Isla.

"I thought that coming here would help. That you could patch things up."

"And now here we are in the mountains, in a snowstorm, in the dark." Isla indicated the scene around them, even though it was plain for James to see.

"I think it's kind of festive," James shrugged and continued eating.

"I think it's freaking me out," Isla muttered.

Clara and Greg came back into the room together. Although Clara's smile was back in place, though it seemed more forced than ever. Like a cracked china doll, Isla thought, beautiful but broken.

"Sorry about that," she trilled. "Just some confusion about the holiday schedule. All sorted now."

"What did they want?" Isla asked innocently. "Your work, I mean."

"Oh, you know," Clara waved her hand vaguely. "Just some last-minute paperwork things. Nothing important."

Greg slipped back into his seat, offering Isla a sheepish smile that was probably meant to be reassuring.

James took his final bite of goose, setting his cutlery down with precision. The soft clink seemed to echo in the tense silence.

Isla studied her sister's face. The shadows under Clara's eyes looked like bruises now, her perfect makeup unable to conceal the strain. Then, carefully, deliberately, she said, "How about we get the men to check the fuse box? Just in case."

Clara's smile froze. Greg's hand jerked, knocking over his water glass. The liquid spread across the tablecloth, destroying the last vestiges of Clara's perfect Christmas dinner setting.

"There's no need," Clara said quickly. Too quickly. "I told you everything is automated. There's no fuse box to check. More wine, anyone?"

But Isla had seen it – that moment of panic when she'd mentioned the fuse box. She caught James's eye again, saw his slight nod. He'd noticed it too.

The wind howled outside, rattling the windows in their frames. The Christmas tree, so magnificent earlier, now loomed in the darkness like a watchful sentinel. Its ornaments caught what little light remained, reflecting distorted versions of their tense faces back at them.

In the darkness, Clara's perfect house didn't seem quite so perfect anymore. And its secrets were beginning to show through the cracks.

"Clara," Isla said in as calm a voice as she could manage, "Why don't you tell us what's going on?"

CHAPTER TEN

The candle flames wavered in a sudden draught, sending their light dancing across Clara's face. She looked like a frightened child caught in a lie – an expression Isla remembered from their childhood, usually preceding an elaborate tale about who really broke Mother's favourite ornament or emptied the Christmas cookie jar.

The memory of those cookies – gingerbread men with crooked icing smiles – hit Isla with unexpected force. She glanced at the elaborate centrepiece: all gilt pinecones and artfully arranged holly. No homemade touches here. Nothing that spoke of genuine family Christmases.

"Going on?" Clara's laugh was too high, too brittle. "Nothing's going on. The power's out, that's all. These things happen."

"In houses with state-of-the-art automated systems?" James's voice was gentle, reasonable. He leaned forward, elbows on the table, his face a mask of concern. The candlelight caught his profile, reminding Isla of how he'd looked at his aunt's funeral — composed, controlled, appropriate. Too appropriate, maybe.

Greg's wine glass clattered against his plate as he reached for it with shaking hands. Some of the liquid slopped over the rim, adding to the spreading stain on the tablecloth. The perfect white linen was now a map of the evening's deterioration – spots of wax, spilled wine, water marks spreading like dark omens.

"The storm," Clara said quickly. "It must be interfering with... with the systems. These smart homes, they're wonderful until they're not." She attempted a light laugh that came out more like a hiccup. "But it's fine. Everything's fine. We just need to wait it out."

Behind her, the Christmas tree loomed in the darkness. Earlier, it had been a vision of holiday perfection, every ornament placed just so. Now its branches seemed to reach toward them like grasping fingers, and the angel looked down with an expression that seemed less beatific and more judgmental.

"The generator should have kicked in by now," James mused, as if to himself. "Unless..."

Greg's head snapped up. "Unless?"

"Well, if there is a generator, we could check it. Might be a simple fix." James smiled, the expression not quite reaching his eyes. "I'm pretty good with mechanical things."

Isla noticed Clara and Greg exchange a quick glance. In the low light, their faces looked like theatrical masks – Clara's fixed in a rictus of forced cheer, Greg's a study in barely contained panic.

"No, no," Clara shook her head, her earrings catching the candlelight. The crystal drops sent tiny rainbows dancing across the table, incongruously festive. "It's much too dangerous to go outside in this weather. We should just wait. The power company will sort it out."

"The power company?" Isla raised an eyebrow. "I thought this place had automated systems for everything. Isn't it all solar powered and self-contained?"

The wind chose that moment to howl particularly loudly, making the windows rattle in their frames. One candle guttered, momentarily plunging half of Clara's face into darkness. Outside, the snow seemed to glow with an eerie light, making the world beyond the windows look alien and hostile.

"Oh, I'm not into all that techy whatever," Clara laughed. "Who knows how it all works? Not me. Not me, that's for sure."

"I'll go," Greg said suddenly. "I'll check the generator."

"Greg, no—" Clara started, but he cut her off.

He stood, his chair scraping against the floor. The sound made Isla think of fingernails on a chalkboard. "No point sitting here in the dark. I can do this. I can."

"Greg—" Clara said again. Her expression was pained.

"I'll help," James offered, already rising. His movement was smooth, practised – like he'd been waiting for this moment. "Two sets of eyes are better than one."

Something flashed across Greg's face, but it was gone before Isla could be sure. The nutcracker statue seemed to watch them with its painted smile, a silent witness to the unfolding scene.

"Well, that's perfect!" Clara's voice was too bright, like costume jewellery trying to pass for diamonds. "While you boys check that out, Isla and I can clear the table. Just like old times, remember? When we used to help Mother with the Christmas dishes?"

The reference to their mother struck Isla like a physical blow. She remembered those dishes – the warmth of the kitchen, the comfortable silence between them as they worked, the way Mother would hum carols under her breath. Nothing like this strained pantomime of family togetherness.

Isla watched as James retrieved his coat from the hall closet, his movements calm and precise in the darkness. There was something almost predatory about his efficiency, she thought, then immediately chided herself. This evening was making her paranoid.

"Be careful out there," Isla called after the men. "It's getting worse."

James turned back, his smile visible. "Don't worry, love. Greg and I will be fine. Won't we, Greg?"

Greg nodded jerkily, already bundled in his coat. "Fine. Yes. Everything's fine."

His repetition of the word made it sound increasingly less convincing.

As the men disappeared into the darkness, Isla heard Greg's muffled voice: "The generator. It's around the back, near the—"

The door closed behind them with a definitive click that seemed to echo in the suddenly too-large house. The sound reminded Isla of a vault being sealed, or a trap being sprung.

Clara immediately began gathering plates, the china rattling in her unsteady hands. "Well! Shall we make a start on these? Though I suppose we can't run the dishwasher..." She gave another of those brittle laughs. "Remember how Mother always said washing up was better by hand, anyway? Built character, she used to say."

"Clara." Isla reached out, stilling her sister's hands. The fine bone china was cold under her fingers, like something long dead. "Stop. Just... stop."

Clara seemed to deflate, her perfect hostess persona cracking like thin ice. Then she straightened her shoulders, lifting her chin. "I don't know what you mean. Now, about these dishes—"

"I mean stop. All of your *family* this, *Mother* that. Stop. You haven't spoken to me in..."

A sudden thud from outside made them both jump and stopped Isla mid-sentence. The sound was quickly swallowed by the wind, but its echo seemed to hang in the air like a warning.

"Probably just slipped in the snow," Clara said quickly. Too quickly. "You know how clumsy Greg can be. Or perhaps you don't..."

Standing in the candlelit dining room, listening to the wind howl around the house, Isla couldn't shake the feeling that something was terribly wrong. The Christmas decorations that had seemed so elegant just hours ago were now more like props in a stage play where everyone had forgotten their lines.

And somehow, she knew this night was about to get much worse.

CHAPTER ELEVEN

The digital display on the smart oven blinked 9:00 in the darkness, its green battery-powered glow casting an eerie pallor across the kitchen. Each passing minute felt like a countdown to something inevitable, the silence between the sisters thick enough to slice with the electric knife Greg had struggled with at dinner.

Clara looked at Isla, breaking the spell.

“Let’s get this cleared. I’m sure they’ll be back shortly.”

Clara continued gathering plates, her movements increasingly frantic. The china clinked dangerously as she stacked plates that shouldn’t be stacked, cutlery clattering into the bowls they’d used for soup. Two kisses. The secret ingredient. Isla tried to shake the thought from her mind.

“Clara, stop,” Isla said. “You’ll break something.”

“Break something?” Clara’s laugh had a hysterical edge that made Isla’s skin prickle. “Oh no, we can’t have that. Everything has to be perfect. Perfect house, perfect dinner, perfect Christmas...” Her voice cracked on the last word, like ice giving way beneath too much weight.

A gust rattled the windows, and both sisters turned instinctively toward the sound. The falling snow was visible in the candlelight that spilled onto the deck, transforming the pristine winter wonderland of earlier into something more menacing.

There was no sign of James or Greg.

There was no sound from the outside world bar the constant howl of the wind.

The kitchen was suddenly too large, too empty. The gleaming surfaces and high-end appliances that Clara had shown off so proudly earlier now seemed to mock them with their silent perfection.

"How long does it take to check a generator?" Isla murmured, more to herself than Clara.

"Oh, you know men and their projects." Clara's attempt at lightness fell flat.

She'd moved on to gathering the unused dessert plates, the ones she'd laid out with such precision hours earlier. Each bore a hand-painted Christmas scene – another detail that now appeared excessive, trying too hard. Miniature families gathered around miniature trees, frozen in perpetual celebration. The dessert would be souring in the powerless refrigerator.

A sharp cry cut through the storm's howl.

"That sounded like—" Isla started toward the window.

"Just the wind," Clara interrupted quickly. Too quickly. "It does that up here. Makes all sorts of strange sounds. Like Mother's old house, remember? How the pipes used to groan on Christmas Eve, and you were convinced it was Santa stuck in the chimney?"

Isla turned to face her sister, really seeing her now in the candlelight. “Stop it, Clara.”

“Stop what?”

“Stop bringing up childhood memories like they’re some kind of shield. Stop pretending everything’s fine when it’s clearly not. Stop—” She broke off as movement caught her eye through the window. A figure emerged from the swirling snow, then disappeared again.

“Is that James or Greg?” Isla asked, pressing her hand against the cold glass.

The frost patterns on the windows were building now, transforming the panes into delicate artwork that would have been beautiful under other circumstances.

Clara had gone still, the dessert plate in her hands reflecting warped candlelight. The painted Christmas scene distorted in the gleam, making the cheerful family gathering look sinister.

“I didn’t see anything.”

Another shout, closer this time. It might have been a name, or a warning, or both. The sound hung in the frigid air like an unfinished prayer.

“We should go out there,” Isla said, already moving toward the hall. The runner beneath her feet, with its elaborate pattern of poinsettias, seemed to shift and writhe in the uncertain light.

“No!” Clara’s voice was sharp with panic. She set down the plate with exaggerated care, as if it might explode at any moment. “I mean, we can’t. It’s too dangerous. The snow, the ice... They’re fine. They're both fine. They'll be back any minute."

As if in answer, the front door burst open. Wind and snow swirled into the hallway, making the candles gutter. The sisters almost collided in the doorway as they raced to see their men.

James stood in the doorway, snow dusting his dark coat like funeral ash. Alone.

"Where's Greg?" Clara's voice was barely a whisper, but it carried all the weight of her mounting fear.

James shook flakes from his hair, his movements deliberate, almost mechanical. "We got separated in the storm. He was right behind me, and then..." He spread his hands helplessly. "I tried to find him, but the visibility's almost zero out there."

"We heard a shout..." Isla began, but Clara cut her off.

"What do you mean, you got separated?" Clara's voice rose. The perfect hostess was gone now, replaced by raw fear. "How do you get separated going to check a generator?"

"It was my fault," James said, his voice heavy with what sounded like regret. "I thought I heard something around the side of the house. Asked Greg to check while I looked at the generator. When I went to find him..." He shrugged, the gesture almost too casual, like an actor who hadn't quite learnt his lines.

Clara was already pulling on her coat, her fingers fumbling with the buttons. "We have to go look for him. He could be anywhere, he could be hurt... He shouldn't be alone. You shouldn't have left him out there. He's..." She shook her head and shut her mouth, trapping whatever secret she'd been about to reveal behind tightly pressed lips.

"Clara, wait." James stepped forward, catching her arm. "We need to be smart about this. Get flashlights, proper gear. Going out there unprepared won't help Greg."

Isla watched her sister sag under the weight of James's logic. Watched James guide Clara to a chair with gentle efficiency. Watched him take control of the situation as naturally as breathing. When had her husband become so practiced at handling crisis situations?

"Where are your emergency supplies?" he asked. "You must have some in a house this well-equipped, in such a ridiculous location." Isla flashed him a sharp look. His tone didn't fit the circumstances. "Clara. Flashlights. Where would they be?"

Clara looked up at him, her face ghostly. All pretence of sophistication had been stripped away. "I... I don't..."

"You don't know?" James's voice was soft, dangerous.

"Greg..." she said. "He deals with all of that. I..."

Isla frowned and looked from Clara to James and then back to her sister again.

"It's a pretty basic but fairly important thing to know, Clara. What if you were up here alone and something..."

Clara was already shaking her head.

"I'm never alone here. Why would I be alone? I can't leave Greg. But look what I did. I sent him out there. I let him go out in this weather and now..." She brought a hand up to her mouth and choked back a sob. "I'm sorry," she said, turning her face away, not wanting her visitors to see her anguish.

Isla took a step towards her sister and then stopped. There was so much distance between them that she couldn't breach it. Instead, she hovered, arm raised for a hug that she couldn't quite bring herself to offer.

Isla glanced at her phone. It was a quarter after nine. Through the windows, the snow continued, erasing footprints and secrets alike.

"How do you not know..." Isla mumbled, as though not wanting to confront Clara. As though she didn't want to face the truth.

An ornament tumbled from the tree with a soft tinkle, rolling across the floor in an escape attempt. It rolled to a stop at Isla's feet – a delicate glass ball painted with a winter scene. It hadn't broken; it had survived the fall. Like everything else in this house, it was perfectly chosen, perfectly placed, and perfectly meaningless. She bent to pick it up, noticing how the painted family inside seemed to watch her with tiny, accusing eyes.

Clara's perfect Christmas was unravelling faster than cheap ribbon, and somehow that seemed more dangerous than Greg being lost in the storm. Her sister had always been like this – building elaborate facades to hide her insecurities. But this time was different. This time reeked of desperation.

"I'm sorry," Clara said, quietly.

"You didn't have to do all this," Isla replied. "You didn't have to invite us."

Clara raised her eyes to meet her sister's and gave her a long, silent stare.

James moved around the room with calculated efficiency, opening drawers and cabinets as if he had every right to search the house. He was taking control, or trying to. Each drawer's slam echoed like an accusation.

"There must be emergency supplies," he said to himself. "No one would be stupid enough to stay up here without basic safety equipment."

The wind changed direction, hurling itself against a different window with renewed fury. The candles flickered.

"Clara..." Isla said.

Clara looked at her and said nothing. She bit her bottom lip in a way that Isla hadn't seen since they were children. The nervous response was unchanged after all the years that had passed.

"You didn't have to..."

"Let's just worry about finding Greg for now," James cut in.

"Greg knows what to do in emergencies," Clara said suddenly, her voice small but fierce. "He's not... he knows what to do. He'll find somewhere safe."

There was something in the way she said it – a protective note that went beyond normal concern. Isla remembered Greg's trembling hands at dinner, the way Clara had guided him so carefully through each social interaction. What wasn't she telling them about her husband? Why were there so many secrets?

Through the windows, the snow had transformed the deck into an arctic landscape. The carefully arranged outdoor furniture, glimpsed earlier through the glass, had become strange shapes under white shrouds.

"I should never have let him go out there," Clara whispered, more to herself than anyone else. "Not in this state. Not with..."

"With what, Clara?" Isla asked. "What aren't you telling us about Greg?"

But Clara just shook her head, pressing her lips together as she had so many times that evening. Another secret to add to the growing pile, like presents under a tree that no one dared unwrap.

This wasn't how Christmas Eve was supposed to be. But then again, nothing about this night was what it seemed.

CHAPTER TWELVE

Clara's face was as pale as the ground outside. Her energy drained, she simply looked at Isla.

"Not now," she said. "Please."

"But..." Isla began.

James took hold of her hand and turned her to face him.

"There will be time for that later," he said. "We need to find a flashlight and go back out there."

Isla's expression crumpled. She turned to the window, where the flurry of swirling snow was just visible in the darkness beyond.

Clara stepped over to the glass, pressing her forehead against it as if she could somehow manifest Greg through sheer force of will.

"We should call the police," Isla said, watching her sister's reflection in the window. Clara's perfect makeup was smeared now, trails of mascara marking her cheeks like tiny rivers of worry.

"No!" Both Clara and James spoke at once, then looked at each other in surprise.

"The roads will be impossible," James continued, yanking open another drawer. "By the time they get here..." He let the sentence hang.

"Impassible?" Isla said.

"Both." James didn't bother turning to look at her.

"Greg doesn't do well with confusion," Clara said softly, her breath fogging the window. "The cold... it'll make everything worse. His medication..."

"What medication?" Isla asked gently.

Clara turned from the window, wrapping her arms around herself. "He's been... struggling. The doctors are still adjusting his dosage. That's why..." She swallowed hard. "That's why this weekend needed to be perfect. No stress. No complications."

"How long?" Isla asked. "How long has he been...?"

"A few months." Clara's voice was barely a whisper. "The doctors say it's temporary. Just stress, they say. Post-traumatic. Pee Tee Ess Dee." She dragged the letters of the acronym out. "But you've seen him, Isla. The tremors, the confusion..." She pressed her fingers to her mouth. "It has to be more than that. He was such a brilliant architect. Now he can barely hold a pencil some days."

James paused in his search, his back to them. "Why didn't you tell us sooner?"

"Tell you what?" Clara's laugh held a hysterical edge. "That my husband's falling apart? That I can barely get him to leave the building most days? That's not exactly the sort of thing you put in a Christmas card, is it? And it's not as though we've kept each other updated about our lives."

The last sentence hit Isla like a snowball to the face. She had been so consumed by her own problems that she hadn't stopped to think that her sister might be going through her own private hell. All those unanswered calls, the declined invitations - she'd assumed Clara was being difficult, distant.

But was Greg's condition the only reason? There was something else in Clara's tone, something that suggested deeper waters.

"I thought..." Clara swallowed hard. "I thought if I could just create one perfect Christmas... If I could show him that everything could still be normal..." Her voice cracked. "But now he's out there alone, and it's all my fault."

James moved his search to the closet where Greg had hung their coats when they first arrived.

"We need to find him soon," he said, voice firm but gentle. "The temperature's dropping."

"We could have managed without electricity until morning," Clara said.

She pulled her phone from her pocket and tapped at the screen with one fierce finger.

"Stupid app. They said it was easy. They said everything we needed was..."

She looked up from the screen at Isla.

"Sorry," she said. "I... I feel so..."

Isla shook her head.

"I feel so useless," Clara completed her sentence. "James, I'll come out with you. I need to look for him. I have to do something."

Much to Isla's surprise, James nodded. "Yes," he said. "Isla should stay here in case Greg finds his way back."

Isla opened her mouth to protest, but Clara cut her off. "Please. Someone needs to be here if... When..." Her voice cracked like thin ice.

"Found one!" James's triumphant cry made both women start. He held up a heavy-duty flashlight from the back of the closet. Testing it, he cast the beam across the living room, catching the reflection of the now-dark Christmas tree in the window. "It's working. That's something, at least. Clara, you'll need to wrap up warm. It's treacherous out there."

Clara nodded, already moving past James to where her designer winter wear hung like party clothes at a funeral. Her crimson dress peeked out beneath the thick down jacket as she struggled with the zipper, her manicured fingers trembling too badly to grip the pull. The transformation from perfect hostess to desperate searcher was jarring - expensive snow boots replacing her stilettos, the pristine white puffer coat covering her festive dress. She looked like a Christmas angel who'd fallen to earth, all elegance lost to necessity.

"What if he's hurt?" she whispered, more to herself than the others. "What if he got confused and wandered into the woods? He gets so lost sometimes, even in familiar places. And with the new medication..."

James helped her with her scarf, wrapping it securely around her neck. "That's why we need to go now, while there's still a chance of following any tracks before the snow covers them completely."

"I should come too," Isla tried again. "Three people searching would be better than—"

"No," James said firmly. "Clara's right. Someone needs to stay here, keep the candles burning. A light in the darkness, something for Greg to find his way back to."

The Christmas tree stood silent witness to their preparation, its unlit branches reaching toward them like beseeching arms.

"Stay by the fire. Keep warm," Clara said, her tone filled with concern.

"Ready?" James asked Clara, holding up the flashlight like a beacon of hope.

Clara nodded, though her eyes were wide with fear. She reached for her sister suddenly, pulling Isla into a fierce hug that smelled of expensive perfume and desperation.

"I'm sorry," she whispered. "About tonight, about everything. I just wanted..."

"Later," Isla said gently, returning the embrace. "We'll talk about everything later. Just find Greg."

James held the front door open, snow immediately swirling into the hallway. The Christmas wreath swung wildly, its red ribbon a violent splash of colour against the white beyond.

Clara stepped out first, immediately disappearing into the swirling darkness until only James's flashlight beam revealed her location.

"Keep warm," James called over his shoulder. "Stay safe."

The storm swallowed his words as the door closed.

Isla stood alone in the hallway, listening to the wind's mournful keen. Everything about this Christmas Eve had gone wrong. The perfect dinner, the elaborate decorations, the carefully maintained facades – all of it crumbling like gingerbread left out overnight.

Isla moved to the window, watching James's flashlight beam cut through the storm like a knife. She pressed her hand against the cold glass, marking it with her warmth, and waited for her world to either right itself or shatter completely.

CHAPTER THIRTEEN

Isla stayed at the window long after the beam of James's flashlight had disappeared into the swirling snow, her breath fogging the glass in small, desperate clouds. The darkness outside seemed absolute now, broken only by the reflection of firelight dancing behind her.

She moved to the armchair by the fire, sinking into its expensive leather. The flames offered the room's only real warmth.

Isla's gaze drifted to the photos on the side table – the happy couple she'd initially mistaken for Clara and Greg. In the dim light, their frozen smiles seemed almost mocking. The more she looked at them, the stranger it seemed that they were on display. Not a single photo of family anywhere – no shots of Clara and Greg's wedding day, no candid moments of the sisters growing up, not even one of those awful formal Christmas portraits their mother had insisted on every year. No Mum. No Dad. Just the same couple, repeated.

When had they become so distant that they didn't even feature in each other's homes anymore? She remembered the last family photo they'd taken together, four Christmases ago. Clara had been wearing that ridiculous reindeer sweater, and they'd both had too much wine, giggling as they tried to get the self-timer to work. That photo should be here somewhere, shouldn't it? Instead of these strangers with their perfect poses and meaningful gazes.

Unless...

Isla let out a long breath, watching it fog in the increasingly cold air. Perhaps it was only jealousy warping her thoughts, making her see mysteries where there were none. After all, Clara had always been the one with expensive taste, with the need to make everything look just so. Maybe these photos were merely part of her desperate attempt at perfection.

We have friends who DO things.

We have friends who travel.

We have friends, and we don't need you.

A distinct thud from upstairs shattered her melancholy thoughts. Her heart stuttered in her chest as she sat frozen in the armchair, straining to hear more. The burning wood popped in the fireplace, the only sound competing with the constant howl of wind outside.

Just the house settling, she told herself. Those perfectly balanced eco-home systems Clara had been so proud to describe earlier must make some noise as they powered down. There was surely a simple explanation for the sound.

Another thud, unmistakable this time.

Isla jumped from her seat and rushed to the window. The snow had swallowed any sign of James and Clara. Their footprints, visible just minutes ago in the glow of James's flashlight, had already been erased by the relentless storm. She was completely, utterly alone.

The fire crackled behind her, and she found herself eyeing the brass poker in its stand. Its gleaming length looked sturdy, defensive. Her fingers twitched toward it before she caught herself. Don't be ridiculous, she thought. This isn't some thriller novel where the heroine investigates strange noises in a dark house during a snowstorm.

And yet.

Her hand closed around the poker's cool metal handle. It was reassuring, solid. Real. She selected one of the larger candles from the mantelpiece, its flame steady despite her trembling hand. The red wax, so festive just hours ago, now reminded her uncomfortably of blood.

Just because she was alone in an isolated house on a mountain during a power cut didn't mean anything sinister was happening. She almost laughed at herself. Almost. But the sound caught in her throat as another creak echoed from above.

The staircase loomed before her, disappearing into absolute darkness. The candlelight barely reached the fourth step. Clara's perfectly arranged garland along the banister cast strange, shifting shadows.

Her heart stuttered.

Each stair creaked beneath her feet despite her careful tread, the sound seeming to echo through the silent house.

At the top, she paused, listening. The master bedroom door stood slightly ajar, a slice of deeper darkness beyond.

Movement caught her eye – but it was just her own reflection in the large mirror at the end of the hall, distorted by candlelight into something barely recognisable.

The master bedroom drew her attention again. Through its doorway, she could make out the shapes of expensive furniture, everything perfectly staged like a show home. The candle's flame reflected off something above the bed.

Keeping the poker ready, she edged into the room. The king-sized bed dominated the space, its crisp white linens undisturbed.

But it was the photo above that stopped her cold.

A wedding photo, elaborate and oversized, showing the same couple from the images downstairs beaming at each other under an arch of white roses. Not Clara and Greg. Not even close.

Isla's mind refused to process what she was seeing. She knew her sister's wedding photos by heart – Clara in that ridiculous meringue of a dress she'd insisted on, Greg looking uncomfortable but happy in his hired suit. This was... this was something else entirely. A different couple. A different wedding. A different life.

She moved closer, raising the candle higher. The bride wore a sleek, modern dress, nothing like Clara's frou-frou choice. The groom was at least a decade older than Greg, with silver threading through his dark hair. Their expressions were perfect, practiced – like everything else in this house.

But why would Clara and Greg have someone else's wedding photo above their bed? It made no sense. None of this made any sense. Unless...

A loud creak from The Pine Room made her spin around, heart thundering. The sound had definitely come from in there. From their room.

Don't, a voice in her head whispered. *Don't be that person in the movie who goes to investigate the strange noise.*

Alone.

The voice sounded suspiciously like her mother's – practical, slightly scolding, usually right.

Isla stood stock still, feeling the weight of the darkness pressing in around her single candle's flame. Her mind raced as rapidly as her heartbeat. Why had she even come upstairs? Candlestick in one hand, poker in the other, like some bizarre Christmas Carol character. What was she expecting? The Ghost of Christmas Present?

Greg. It must be Greg. Could he have found his way back in somehow? Through a window, perhaps, or a back door they didn't know about? If he had, he might need help. That's what she had stayed behind for: to be here for her brother-in-law. She took a deep breath, trying to steady herself, and reminded herself that she didn't believe in ghosts of Christmas past, present, or future. This was reality, not some Dickensian nightmare.

The poker felt heavier in her grip as she crossed the hall, each step measured and careful on the polished wood floor. The Pine Room's door opened silently on its expensive hinges, revealing the fairy lights they'd abandoned earlier – dead now, like tiny corpses draped across the window frame. Their lifeless bulbs seemed to watch her, waiting.

Another creak. From the bathroom.

"Greg?" she whispered, though she knew in her heart he wasn't there. Her voice sounded thin and frightened, even to her own ears.

The bedroom was empty, the perfectly arranged pillows untouched. The bathroom door was closed. Had it been closed when they left? She couldn't remember. To open it, she would have to put down either the candlestick or the poker. In a snap decision, she stood the candlestick on the bedside table, keeping a tight hold of her only means of defence.

Her hand shook as she reached for the bathroom door handle, making her shadow dance wildly on the wall behind her. The handle turned easily, smoothly expensive, but the door wouldn't budge. Not locked – she could hear the mechanism working – but something was blocking it from the other side.

There's someone in there. On the floor.

Isla tried to sweep each thought aside as it entered her mind, but they kept coming, relentless as the storm outside.

Someone fell. That thud...

Her brain was trying to work out what had happened from the minimal information it had, creating scenarios each more terrifying than the last.

Isla pushed harder, pressing her shoulder against the solid wood. Something scraped across the tiled floor inside, a sound that made her teeth ache. The door gave way slightly – just enough for her to see the bathroom mirror, reflecting nothing but darkness back at her.

She looked down into the space she had made between door and frame.

"Hello?" she whispered. Her throat was desert dry. She cleared it and tried again, forcing steel into her voice. "Is someone there?"

Without the candle, she could see nothing in the wedge of blackness. The silence pressed against her eardrums like cotton wool.

Taking another deep breath, Isla set the poker against the wall, within reach, and grabbed the candlestick. The flame guttered slightly as she moved. Bending slightly, she peered in through the gap, holding the light before her like a shield.

She recoiled in horror.

There was a body lying on the floor.

CHAPTER FOURTEEN

Isla scrambled backward across the lush carpet, her heel catching on the rug, sending her sprawling. The candlestick tilted dangerously in her grip as she fell, hot wax spattering across her hand. She barely registered the pain, focused only on keeping the flame from igniting the expensive carpeting while putting as much distance as possible between herself and whatever lay beyond that bathroom door.

Her back hit the bed frame with enough force to knock the breath from her lungs. The candle's flame danced wildly, casting grotesque shadows across the walls. Shadows that looked like bodies. Like corpses. Like —

Stop it, she commanded herself, though her heart continued to thunder against her ribs.

Think. Breathe. Think.

She forced herself to take one deep breath, then another. The carpet beneath her hands was thick and soft, grounding her in reality. The flame steadied as her hands stopped shaking quite so violently.

Look again, the rational part of her brain insisted. *Really look.*

But terror kept her frozen in place, her eyes fixed on the partially open bathroom door. From this angle, she could see just a slice of what lay beyond – a dark shape on the white tile floor, fabric draped across it like a shroud...

But this fabric was black, and it looked strangely familiar.

The cardigan.

The realisation hit her like a splash of cold water. Her cardigan. The one she'd thrown over the tacky Santa decoration because its painted-on smile had creeped her out.

A hysterical laugh bubbled up in her throat. She'd nearly set fire to a house worth more than she'd earn in a decade because of a Christmas decoration. If Clara could see her now...

But Clara was outside in the snow, fighting through the bitter cold with James.

And she was alone in the house, hearing ghosts in every creak.

She knew she should go back downstairs. Should wait by the fire for the others to return. Should pretend she hadn't seen the wedding photo of strangers in what was supposed to be her sister's bedroom.

She used the bed to pull herself up, her legs still shaking slightly. What a fool she'd been, coming up here alone, letting her imagination run wild like...

"Claaaaaa."

The sound drifted up from downstairs, stopping her thoughts cold. A low groan, barely audible over the constant howl of the wind.

She stood perfectly still, wondering if she'd imagined it. The house was playing tricks on her, surely. The wind in the eaves, the settling of expensive timbers, the...

"Help..."

This time, there was no mistaking it.

A voice.

Greg's voice.

And he sounded hurt.

Isla ran for the stairs, taking them two at a time, despite the danger of missing her footing in the poor lighting. Greg stood in the entrance, leaning heavily against the wall. Blood matted his hair.

"Greg! What happened? Where are the others?"

He tried to focus on her face, his pupils uneven.

"James," he managed before his knees buckled.

Then his eyes rolled back, and Isla barely managed to catch him as he crumpled to the floor. She staggered under Greg's weight, just managing to break his fall. The candlestick wobbled dangerously in her grip as she tried to lower him without dropping it or setting anything alight. Greg's head lolled against her shoulder, his skin frighteningly cold where it touched her neck.

"Greg?" She shifted, trying to find a way to set the candle down safely. "Greg, can you hear me?"

No response. His breathing was shallow but steady – unconscious, not...

She couldn't finish that thought.

The front door still stood open behind them, letting in swirling snow and bitter cold. The wind howled through the gap. She needed to close it, but she couldn't bring herself to leave Greg, even for those few steps. What if he stopped breathing? What if he...?

Focus, she told herself firmly. *One problem at a time.*

She managed to set the candlestick on the floor beside them, her hands shaking as she tried to make it stable. Greg's pulse fluttered under her fingers as she checked his neck – steady but weak. The blood in his hair had begun to dry, dark and crusty. Head wounds always bled dramatically, she reminded herself. It might look worse than it was.

"Greg," she tried again, gently patting his cheek. "Can you hear me? What happened?"

His eyelids fluttered but didn't open. His lips moved, forming words she couldn't quite catch.

She leaned closer. "What?"

He mumbled, but his words made even less sense than earlier. Before she could press him further, his head slumped to the side again.

Isla eased out from under him.

"I'll be right back," she whispered to Greg's unconscious form, though she wasn't sure why she was whispering.

The few steps seemed endless, but she forced herself to move quickly. The heavy door took all her strength to close against the wind, and when it finally clicked shut, the sudden absence of the storm's howl was almost as unsettling as the noise had been. The house felt too quiet now, too still.

Next, she moved over to grab one of Clara's perfectly arranged sofa cushions. Her sister would be horrified at the thought of bloodstains on her expensive fabric, but it was *Greg*. Greg was more important than keeping the accessories clean.

Kneeling beside him again, she gently lifted his head to slide the cushion underneath. In the barely adequate light, she carefully examined the wound. The blood was matted at the back of his skull, creating a dark patch in his hair. He could have slipped on the ice, she reasoned, fallen backward instead of forward. That would explain the location of the injury. But something about the shape of it - the way the blood had congealed - it felt wrong.

She pushed the thought away. There had to be a logical explanation. People didn't just get attacked on Christmas Eve in luxury mountain homes. Why would she even think that?

Still shaken up from the attack of the Santa model. Things that go bump in the night. Ghosts of Christmas Whatever.

But what if that *was* what had happened?

James was out there right now with Clara, searching for Greg. What if they ran into whatever – whoever – had hurt the man who was lying beside her?

Stop it, she told herself firmly. *You're letting your imagination run away again.*

Just like with the Santa upstairs.

Just like with the couple in the photo. The wedding photo.

But the Santa had been easily explained. This injury, the location of it, the way Greg had stumbled in alone...

What if James and Clara were hurt, too? What if they needed help?

Greg's wound kept drawing her attention, raising questions she wasn't sure she wanted answered.

First things first.

Greg was cold.

She should try to warm him up, get him out of these wet clothes. But moving him seemed dangerous – what if the head injury was worse than it looked? What if she made things worse?

She settled for removing his snow-covered boots and jacket, then retrieved a throw from the sofa to cover him. His skin was like frozen chicken where she touched it. Whatever had happened out there in the storm, he'd been exposed to the elements for too long.

"I don't know what to do, Greg," she whispered, arranging the blanket up around his shoulders, beneath his chin. "I don't know how to help any of you."

She needed to get him closer to the fire, but dragging an unconscious man across the expensive carpeting seemed impossible.

Isla looked at her phone again. How long had it been since James and Clara left? How long should she wait before... before what? What could she possibly do to help them?

She was trapped here, as surely as if the storm had locked them in. Trapped with an unconscious man who might or might not have been attacked, waiting for two people who might or might not be in danger.

"Please wake up," she whispered to Greg. "Please help me understand what's happening."

But Greg remained stubbornly unconscious, and the storm continued to rage outside, and somewhere in that swirling darkness were the two people she loved most in the world.

And she had never felt more useless in her life.

CHAPTER FIFTEEN

The candlelight cast a surreal glow over Greg's unconscious face as Isla knelt beside him, her mind cycling through increasingly desperate options. She couldn't leave him to go for help. Couldn't move him closer to the fire alone. Couldn't do anything except sit here in the growing cold and worry.

She stared at the phone in her hand; its screen showed a weak network connection. Even if Clara and James were out in the swirling snow, they might have enough signal to receive a call. She had to at least try. Let them know Greg was back. Tell them he was – mostly – all right.

She paused and then tried Clara's number first. The phone actually rang, surprising her – but then she heard the answering echo from the kitchen. Following the sound, candlelight bobbing with each step, Isla found Clara's phone lying abandoned on the counter next to half-empty glasses of mulled wine and badly stacked dinnerware.

There was no trace of whatever had crashed and broken earlier; all signs of it had been confined to the bin. Dinner seemed such a long time ago, and awkward as it was, Isla would have given anything to be sitting at the table with the full party intact again.

Contacting Clara was out of the question. Her phone with its lock screen image of her and Greg in an embrace that almost rivalled that of the mysterious photo couple was here. Useless.

James, then.

She jabbed at his contact number, more urgently now. One ring. Two rings. Three...

"Hi, this is James Duvall. Leave a message."

Isla lowered the phone slowly, staring at its dimly lit screen. Hearing his voice was reassuring, even though it was a message that he had recorded years ago, before the two of them had even met.

She should say something. Let James know what was happening. If he didn't have signal now, it might pick up. The phone would trill out the alert as soon as the network connected.

Without thinking, she spoke.

"James, it's me." Isla paused, unsure how to phrase what came next. "Listen, I don't know if you'll get this before you come back, but Greg's here. He's... well, he's hurt, but he's alive." She winced at how that sounded. "No, I mean, he's fine. He will be fine. Just come back as soon as you can. Try that generator again on your way in? It's getting cold in here..." She trailed off, then added quickly, "Don't worry Clara. He's breathing fine. Just... just come back."

She clicked the phone closed, ending the call, and cursed herself under her breath.

What a dumb message. I should have thought it through.

It *was* getting cold, though. She hadn't thought about it until she said the words. When Greg had come in, the door had been open for too long, letting the night's chill in with him. The fire was dying down, and it seemed as though the fire was all they had.

Isla looked around for signs of radiators, but there were none to be seen. *Underfloor heating*, she remembered Clara saying.

No radiators, then. There was, though, a basket of logs beside the fireplace. She pulled one from the heap, tentatively edged towards the fire, and tossed it unceremoniously on top.

Her hand reached out to find a poker, and she realised she had left it upstairs, next to the fallen Santa.

It could stay there.

The fire would surely be fine.

Isla extended her palms, warming them in the dwindling heat from the flames.

All they needed were marshmallows to toast, or maybe chestnuts to roast, and perhaps it would feel more festive again.

Isla sucked in a breath and blew it out through her puckered lips. They needed a lot more than that, and she knew it.

There was one more question playing on Isla's mind: Should she call the police?

What would she even tell them? That her brother-in-law had stumbled in from the snow with a head wound that might or might not be suspicious? That her sister and husband were out looking for him, not knowing he was already here?

Greg's breathing had steadied somewhat, becoming deeper and more regular. She knelt beside him again, studying the wound as best she could in the low light. The more she looked at it, the more she could convince herself it was just a fall. People did slip on ice. Did bang their heads. Especially in weather like this.

Just like she'd convinced herself there was a body in the bathroom, when it had only been that tacky Santa figure.

She was letting her imagination run wild again. Too much mulled wine and champagne earlier, though the blackout and Greg's disappearance had certainly sobered her up.

James and Clara would be back soon, she told herself firmly. They'd laugh about all this tomorrow, over Christmas breakfast. Clara would fuss about the bloodstains on her cushion, Greg would be embarrassed about falling, and...

And she wouldn't mention the fallen Santa.

Or the wedding photo upstairs.

Or any of the other little things that didn't quite add up.

She needed something positive to think about. She needed something a little more festive and a little less sinister.

"Hot chocolate," Isla murmured to herself. "We need hot chocolate."

She could heat it on the fire, like her mum used to. The sugar and warmth would do Greg good when he woke up, and hopefully by then James and Clara would have returned. Or at least they might have heard her message.

Isla made her way to the kitchen, then stopped, looking at her phone, still clutched in her hand. She'd been wandering around with an open flame when she had a perfectly good torch in her pocket. Caught up in the drama of it all, she supposed - acting like some Gothic heroine with her candlestick. Time to be more practical.

The phone's beam was arguably better than candlelight anyway, more focused as she searched through cupboards and drawers for a pan, mugs, and spoon. The third drawer she tried stuck slightly, and as she pulled harder, she saw why - a glossy brochure was wedged at the back.

"*Welcome to our little place in the mountains*," read the cover in elegant script.

Isla's heart seemed to stutter as she pulled it free. Inside were pages of detailed instructions - how to work the heating, where to find the emergency generator, the location of the nearest grocery store. An entire section was devoted to the smart house features Clara had been so proud to demonstrate earlier.

Isla's hands trembled as she turned the pages. The Morrisons' mountain retreat came with everything - state-of-the-art kitchen appliances, underfloor heating, even a wine cellar stocked with local vintages that guests were welcome to sample. Every luxury imaginable, all outlined in precise detail with contact numbers for the owners prominently displayed on each page.

The owners.

Not Clara and Greg.

The *actual* owners.

Of course, Isla had her suspicions when she saw those photos in the other room - the happy couple who definitely weren't her sister and brother-in-law beaming from their frames. But photos in the living area were one thing. That giant wedding portrait above what was supposed to be Clara and Greg's bed? That was something else entirely. If she had been less concerned about chasing the Ghost of Christmas Whatever, she would have had more time to stop and think about it.

This clearly wasn't Clara's house, after all.

The perfect show home with its perfect Christmas decorations and perfect everything was just... what? A rental? An Airbnb? Isla cast her eyes down to the brochure again. The Morrisons' Mountain Retreat.

Isla reached out her hand to steady herself against the countertop, almost dropping her phone.

Why lie about it? Why not just tell her and James that they'd rented somewhere nice for Christmas? It wasn't as if Isla would have judged her sister for not owning a luxury mountain home.

Unless there was more to it.

Unless this was part of something bigger.

The phone call earlier that Clara had claimed was from work. The way Greg had been acting all evening, even before he'd disappeared into the storm. PTSD, Clara had said. From what?

And then Greg's mysterious accident.

And Clara and James were still out there in the snowstorm.

Her phone rang, making her drop the brochure.

James's name lit up the screen.

"James?" Her voice sounded small in the empty kitchen.

But all she could hear was the howl of wind, pierced by a sound that might have been a sob.

Then the line went dead.

CHAPTER SIXTEEN

Isla bent to pick the brochure from off the floor; its glossy pages slipped against her trembling fingers. The emergency generator section was detailed, complete with colour-coded diagrams. According to the Morrisons' instructions, it was a simple enough process – first use the app to trigger a reset. Should that fail, the user should locate the unit behind the house, press the reset button, wait thirty seconds, then flip the master switch.

The beam of her phone light caught her reflection in the darkened window as she considered her options. She could bundle up in warm clothes, venture out into the storm... but that would mean leaving Greg unconscious and alone. What if he woke up confused, maybe even delirious? What if he needed help, and she wasn't there? The image of him lying helpless in the dark made her stomach clench.

She had a responsibility to him, and she had a responsibility to Clara. Whatever was going on. Whatever reason her sister had for lying to her and James. Clara was still family, and so was Greg. There was no way she was going to leave him.

No. She would stick to her original plan. Make the hot chocolate. Stay by Greg's side. Surely Clara and James would be back any minute. They had to be getting cold out there, had to have realised by now that continuing to search was futile in this weather.

James must have heard the voicemail that she left.

Unless something had happened to them, too.

It was too chilling to think about that. Isla swayed, unsteady on her feet.

Nothing had happened. They were fine. They would be back by the time she had boiled the milk.

That sound on the phone... that sob.

If it had been Clara crying, it was hardly surprising. She must be frantic about Greg, imagining all sorts of terrible scenarios, while he lay here on their borrowed floor in their borrowed house.

Borrowed. Rented.

Isla glanced down at the brochure again. The Morrisons' contact information was right there, their emergency number printed in bold on every page. They probably had protocols for situations like this. Power outages in mountain storms couldn't be that uncommon.

But it was Christmas Eve. She didn't want to call the owners out on a night like this. The Morrisons no doubt had better things to do. When it came down to the facts, none of them had yet even tried to follow the instructions in the manual to get the generator online. No. She would have to wait.

Hot chocolate. That's what she'd come in here for. Something warm and sweet and comforting, like her mother used to make. She could almost hear Mum's voice: "Hot chocolate solves everything."

The kitchen drawers yielded a heavy-based pan that would work on the fire. In the pantry, she found cocoa powder and sugar. Her hands shook slightly as she added milk from the fridge into the pan, spilling a few drops onto the counter.

She could call James again while she worked. Leave another message. But what would she say? "By the way, Clara, I know this isn't your house and I found the owners' manual and why didn't you just tell us the truth?"

Why hadn't she?

What was she trying to hide?

When Isla had walked into the *little place* earlier in the evening, hadn't she been impressed by what Clara had bought with their mother's money? Hadn't she thought that, yes, Clara had made something of herself? She wasn't still skipping around from rental to rental, switching jobs every few months, floating around with no purpose in life.

Hadn't she thought Clara deserved the inheritance?

And now? Hadn't that changed?

The fact of it was, she had believed Clara. She had wanted to believe Clara. She had wanted to believe that Clara had taken their mother's money and invested it in something worthwhile rather than...

Isla swallowed hard. Better to wait. Better to focus on practical things - hot chocolate, warmth, comfort. The truth could wait until they were all safely inside, until Greg was conscious, and Clara had stopped crying and James...

The wind hurled itself against the windows with renewed fury, making the glass rattle in its frames. Isla jumped, nearly dropping the pan.

She made her way back into the living area and crouched with her face just above Greg's. She could hear Greg's steady breathing, each exhale a reminder that at least he was alive. At least he was safe. His chest rose slightly and fell again, rose and fell.

Isla nodded and smiled.

Everything was fine.

She should concentrate on making hot chocolate. On keeping the fire going. On practical, useful things that didn't involve wondering why her sister would lie about a house, or be crying in a snowstorm, or why her brother-in-law had a wound on the back of his head that looked less and less like a fall, the more she thought about it.

She wouldn't think about it. Not yet.

Isla reached out to smooth Greg's hair back from his forehead. His skin was clammy under her touch, too cool despite the fire's warmth. She lingered there, this gentle contact somehow making her feel less alone in the vast, dark house.

Making her way to the fireplace, she settled the pan carefully among the glowing embers, pushing aside the log she had added. The flames danced beneath it, reminding her of winter evenings long ago, when power cuts meant adventure rather than anxiety. She and her mother would make hot chocolate by firelight, a special treat that transformed darkness into magic.

"Careful now," Mum would say, guiding Isla's small hands as she stirred the milk. "Nice and slow, that's it." The metal spoon would scrape against the bottom of the pan, making sure nothing stuck or scorched. It was a delicate art, one that required patience and attention.

Clara would hover at the edges of these moments, just beyond the firelight's reach. Too young, Mum always said, to be near the flames. Too little to handle hot pans and marshmallows on toasting forks. "Your turn will come," Mum would promise, but somehow Clara's time never quite arrived.

Isla watched the milk begin to steam, remembering how Clara would crane her neck to see past them, trying to join their little cooking ritual. How many times had she stood there, watching her older sister and mother share something in which she couldn't take part?

No, that couldn't be right. Clara had been Mum's favourite - everyone knew that. The baby of the family, the one who could do no wrong. Isla must be misremembering, painting herself as the chosen one when it had always been Clara.

But the memory was so clear: Clara's small face pale while Isla and Mum laughed together by the fire, sharing the secret language of cooking and comfort that Clara never quite learned to speak.

The milk bubbled, pulling Isla back to the present. She added the cocoa and sugar, stirring carefully just as her mother had taught her. The rich smell filled the air, a promise of warmth and sweetness in this cold, dark night.

Behind her, Greg's breathing remained steady and deep. In the firelight, his face looked younger somehow, vulnerable. Like Clara used to look, watching from the sidelines while Isla and Mum...

Stop it, she told herself firmly.

She was doing it again - seeing patterns that weren't there, creating mysteries where none existed.

The hot chocolate simmered, and Isla pushed the unsettling thoughts away. She had more immediate concerns than childhood memories that might or might not be accurate. Greg was hurt. James and Clara were still out in the storm. And somewhere in this borrowed house, buried beneath lies and pretence, was a truth she wasn't sure she wanted to uncover.

CHAPTER SEVENTEEN

Isla ladled the hot chocolate carefully into two mugs, the rich aroma filling the darkened room with memories of simpler times. She left some in the pan, nestled in the embers to stay warm for when Clara and James returned.

It wouldn't be long. What she thought she had heard must have been her mind playing tricks on her again.

"Here we go," she murmured, settling back beside Greg. She set his drink on the table next to the photo of the Morrisons in Paris. "I probably shouldn't give you any until you're properly awake, but it's here if you want it." She cupped her own mug between her palms, letting the warmth seep into her fingers.

The firelight shone on Greg's face. In the years she'd known him, they'd never really spoken. He'd always been calm, letting Clara fill the silence with her endless chatter. But there had been moments, glimpses of someone thoughtful beneath the surface. Someone who watched and noticed things.

"You know," Isla said, taking another sip of hot chocolate, "I always thought you were perfect for Clara. A little... quiet. A little steady. But that's exactly what she needed after all those wild boyfriends, all that drama." She studied his unconscious face, remembering the way he'd look at Clara when she was talking, like every word mattered. "I used to be jealous, if I'm being honest. Of what you two had. Have."

She shifted, adjusting the cushion under his head. "Clara's always been the golden one, hasn't she? Younger, prettier, kinder too if I'm being really honest. The way she reaches out, makes an effort. Like tonight - this whole Christmas fantasy she created. And here's me, thinking the worst of her for not being completely upfront about the house."

The fire popped, sending sparks up the chimney. "But did she actually say it was yours? I've been sitting here getting worked up about lies and deception, but... she just said the *little place in the mountains*, didn't she? It is your place, for Christmas at least. You must have spent a fortune renting it for us."

She took another slow sip of hot chocolate, letting the warmth spread through her chest. The more she thought about it, the more she felt ashamed of her quick judgement. Clara had always tried so hard - too hard, maybe, but wasn't that better than not trying at all? Like Isla herself, who couldn't remember the last time she'd initiated contact with her sister.

Here they were, in this beautiful house on Christmas Eve, and she was constructing elaborate theories about deception when, really, Clara had just wanted to give them all a perfect holiday. That was Clara all over - grand gestures, big heart, endless hope that this time, this effort would bridge the gap between them.

"You know," she said softly, "I always wondered what you really thought of our family. All our drama and complications. Must have been quite a shock, marrying into this mess." She laughed quietly. "Though I suppose every family has its secrets."

Greg's breathing remained steady, but she could have sworn his eyelids wavered slightly at the word 'secrets'.

Isla drained the last of her hot chocolate and set her empty mug on the side table, next to Greg's untouched one. As she placed it down, her elbow caught one of the framed photos - the Morrisons beaming on some tropical beach. She caught it before it could topple backward, straightening it with careful fingers. Such a happy couple, she thought, wondering what they'd make of the drama unfolding in their perfect mountain retreat tonight.

She moved back to Greg's side, kneeling beside him on the thick carpet. Her fingers ghosted over the wound on the back of his head, barely touching the matted hair.

"It's so dangerous out there," she whispered, more to herself than to him. "Please come back soon, both of you. I'm doing my best here, Greg, but I don't... I'm not sure what I'm supposed to do."

The fire crackled behind her, casting their shadows long against the wall. Outside, the wind's howl had taken on an almost human quality, like someone crying in the distance.

She stroked Greg's hair back from his forehead, her touch gentle as a mother's. Her other hand reached into her pocket for her phone, as if by its own volition. It was silent. No more calls. No more sobs in the darkness.

"You know," she said softly, her fingers tracing the line of his cheek, "I really thought I was helping her. Clara was so... scattered. So unsettled. Job to job, place to place, never putting down roots. When Mum left everything to me, I thought..." She swallowed hard. "I thought giving it all to Clara would force her to grow up. To take responsibility. To have the life she deserved."

How many Christmases had they missed? How many years of silence because she'd thought she knew what was best for her little sister?

Greg stirred slightly under her touch, his lips moving. "Help... her..."

"Yes," Isla whispered, her voice catching. "That's exactly what I was trying to do. But all it did was push her away. Three years of not speaking. Three years of..." She broke off, realising she was crying. When had she started crying?

"I should have just told her," Isla continued, her thoughts spilling out like the tears she couldn't seem to stop. "Should have explained why I did it.

But I was so sure I knew best, so certain that was what she needed. And now look at us - playing pretend in a borrowed house on Christmas Eve, while the storm..." She glanced toward the window, where the snow swirled like lost ghosts seeking shelter.

Greg's breathing had changed slightly, becoming more shallow, more irregular.

"Help her," he mouthed again, this time the words sounding more formed. Still, he didn't open his eyes. He was talking in his sleep, repeating what Isla had said.

The fire snapped loudly. In a moment of startled movement, Isla could have sworn Greg's eyes opened, just for a second. But when she looked again, his face was as calm as before.

She was losing it. The stress, the worry, the guilt - it was all becoming too much. She needed James and Clara to come back. Needed this night to make sense again.

Greg's lips moved again, but this time, no sound came out. Isla leaned closer, her ear almost touching his mouth, straining to hear. But there was only the wind's endless howl and the fire's hungry crackle and her own racing thoughts, tumbling over each other like snow in the storm.

A blast of arctic air hit her face as the front door crashed open. Isla looked up to see Clara stagger through, slamming it behind her and throwing the lock with trembling hands. She pressed herself against the wood, her chest heaving, her perfect Christmas outfit now soaked below the thick white jacket.

"Clara!" Isla scrambled to her feet. "What happened? Where's James?"

Her sister's hair was wild, tangled and damp with snow, plastered to her face in wet strands. There were red marks on her neck, just visible above the collar of her jacket.

"Don't," Clara gasped, holding up one hand to keep Isla back. Her eyes were wide with terror as they darted around the room, finally landing on Greg's unconscious form. "Oh no. Greg..."

"He's alive," Isla said quickly. "He's breathing. Clara, what's going on? Where's James?"

CHAPTER EIGHTEEN

Without even speaking further to Isla, Clara swept up the candlestick and rushed to the back door, checking its lock with frantic movements.

"We have to lock all the windows," she called through from the back entrance. "Every door. Every possible entry point."

"Clara, stop!" Isla grabbed her sister's arm. "What's happening? Where's James? What if he needs to get in?"

Clara darted back into the room and stood still. She stared at her sister, her mouth falling open slightly.

"Isla..." she began.

"James..." Greg said, his voice one long sigh.

Clara's eyes flicked over to her husband.

"Stop," Isla said, reaching out and putting her hand onto Clara's arm. "What about...? Is someone out there? You can't leave James out there with..."

She cut the sentence off.

Clara's eyebrows shot up as Isla's face showed the first traces of realisation dawning.

"No!" Isla said, recoiling. "No! What are you trying to say?"

Clara glanced down at Greg, who appeared to have slipped back into his transient darkness, and jerked away.

"Let me..." Clara started. "Help me secure the house first."

Clara dashed past Isla, continuing her manic circuit of the house. She tested each window lock, each door handle, muttering under her breath as she went. Her hair hung in wet ropes around her face.

Isla watched her, then turned to look at Greg.

"She wants to shut him out," she whispered conspiratorially. "On Christmas Eve. Can you believe it?"

Greg was silent apart from his deep, laboured breaths.

Finally, Clara appeared back in the room. Even from a few feet away, even in the dim light, Isla could see a purple flower of a bruise forming on her neck.

She had her phone in her hand, retrieved from the kitchen counter where she had left it abandoned earlier.

"I have to call the police," Clara said, her breath shallow and fast. "I'm so sorry, Isla, but..."

"No," Isla said. "You're mistaken. Whatever you think happened, James... He wouldn't."

Clara crouched by Greg's side, checking him over. Her fingers found the soft, damp depression on the back of his head.

"Oh, no!" she said. "Isla! Did you know about this?"

"Whoever attacked Greg must have attacked you, too. It must be hard to see out there, in all that snow. It could be quite confusing. White everywhere. The ground, the air." Isla was clutching at straws.

"Isla. Please. Do me a favour and sit down. In fact, please throw another log onto the fire and then sit down. We need to keep it going."

Without argument, Isla picked up another hefty log from the basket and threw it into the embers. She reached out for the pan of hot chocolate and set it onto the stone fireplace. It wasn't the time to offer Clara a warming mug. She had to do what she was told.

Clara nodded reassuringly and indicated towards the sofa.

When Isla was sitting, she looked at her sister with terror in her eyes.

"Clara." Isla kept her voice steady despite her racing heart. "Tell me what happened out there."

"James." Clara's voice broke on the name. "James happened." She stroked Greg's face with trembling fingers, the gesture tender despite her obvious fear. "He wasn't looking for Greg at all. He knew exactly where he was going because he... he..."

"No." Isla said. "James wouldn't—"

"He tried to kill me!" Clara's voice rose sharply, making Greg stir. She immediately lowered it to a whisper. "That cliff beyond the house? He said we should check there for Greg. Then he... he just..." She pressed her hand to her mouth, shoulders shaking.

Isla slid forward off the sofa and sank to her knees beside her sister. "Start from the beginning. Please."

Clara drew a shuddering breath. "At first, we headed off together. We were both calling Greg's name. It was impossible to see more than a few feet ahead of us, though. The snow is savage. I always thought it was beautiful, but tonight, it was brutal. We headed around the back, and then onto the road. I couldn't even see footprints. Oh, good gracious, it was a mistake coming here." She took in another breath, centring herself.

"When it seemed like we were getting nowhere, we split up to cover more ground. James suggested it. Said we'd find Greg faster that way. I went toward the trees while he checked behind the house." She touched the bruises on her neck. "Or at least he said that's what he was going to do. He came up behind me. Started talking about *fairness* and... and then he just grabbed me. I didn't realise it, but I was on the edge of an outcrop. I couldn't see, I didn't know. He backed me up, pushed me toward the edge."

"But why would he—"

"I fought back," Clara continued, as if Isla hadn't spoken. "I managed to break free, but he... the look in his eyes, Isla. I've never seen anyone look like that."

Isla's mind raced back through the evening. James's calm when Greg disappeared.

"He's strong, though, your husband," Clara said with a dark smile. "I couldn't hold him off. He lunged at me, and I couldn't keep my balance. His hands were around my throat, so tight. I thought he was going to choke me, right there. But instead, he shoved me. Pushed me back with so much force I couldn't stop myself from falling."

Clara's eyes brimmed with sadness. She was stroking Greg's hair with one hand, wiping at her tears with the other.

"Some Christmas this turned out to be," she sobbed.

Regaining her composure, Clara looked Isla dead in the eye. "I have to call the police. You see that, don't you? I'm so sorry."

Isla leaned back against the side table on which sat Greg's hot chocolate, now cold, and the images of the Morrisons.

"Greg came back a while ago," she said slowly. "Confused, bleeding. He tried to say something about James before he passed out."

Clara's head snapped up. "What did he say?"

"Just James's name. Then he collapsed. I've been trying to keep him warm, made hot chocolate..." It all seemed so absurd now – playing nurse with hot chocolate while James was out there trying to...

"Did you call anyone?" Clara's eyes darted to the windows, now black mirrors reflecting their frightened faces.

"I tried you both. James actually called back, but there was just... just the wind. And what sounded like crying."

"That was probably when..." Clara swallowed hard. "When I was struggling. The snow was so deep it cushioned my fall. The drop wasn't nearly as high as James must have thought. I was winded, but other than that, I think I'm pretty much all right."

Isla nodded.

"I played dead, though. I thought, you know, if he thinks he's killed me. If he believes the fall was enough, he'll leave me alone."

"Confirm the kill," Isla muttered.

"What?" Clara said, incredulous.

"Sorry," Isla said. "It's what James always says when we watch those tacky straight to streaming thriller movies. The assailant never confirms the kill, and the victim can somehow make their getaway. Or get their revenge."

Clara gave Isla one long stare.

"This isn't a thriller movie, Isla. This is our lives. James tried to kill me. Your husband tried to kill me." She moved her hand around to Greg's wound again. "And I don't think I have to be much of a detective to figure out that this is probably James's handiwork too."

"James," Greg said again. His eyes blinked.

Isla gulped hard. The aftertaste of the hot chocolate was suddenly unpleasant. The festive vibes had melted away.

"James," Greg moaned, his upper body moving from the floor.

Clara whipped her head around to follow Greg's gaze.

There, standing at the window, was James.

And he looked unhinged.

CHAPTER NINETEEN

Isla's heart stopped as she turned, following Clara's horrified stare. James was standing at the window, his face highlighted by the firelight against the darkness outside. Snow clung to his coat in thick patches, and his eyes gleamed in the dim light, fury etched into every line of his face. His hands, pressed against the glass, left smudges on the frosted pane. The storm outside seemed to pulse in sync with his rage.

"Oh my," Isla breathed, unable to tear her eyes away. She was rooted to the spot, her mind reeling between disbelief and dread. He was supposed to be her husband, the person she trusted most, and now he was on the other side of that window—looking like he was deciding whether to break through it.

"Isla!" Clara's whisper was sharp, desperate. "We need to move. We can't just sit here."

But Isla was frozen, her eyes locked on James, trying to reconcile the man she knew with the monster staring back. Was it really him? Could he be capable of this?

"Isla, please!" Clara grabbed her by the shoulders, shaking her so hard that Isla snapped out of her stupor. Clara's bruised neck was a cruel reminder of everything she had just heard. It was real—every word Clara had said, the terror on her face. This was no mistake.

As if reading her mind, James slammed his hand against the window, making them both jump. The sharp sound shattered the silence, and Greg let out a guttural groan from the floor. Clara bent to him, cradling his head as she glanced frantically between Isla and the window.

"What do we do?" Isla whispered, her voice barely audible over the roaring wind outside. She felt like a child, lost and afraid, unable to comprehend the danger. She wanted James to explain, to tell her it was all a misunderstanding, but there was no explanation that would make sense of the madness in his eyes.

"We need to move," Clara ordered, her voice stronger now, taking charge.

She stood and pulled Isla to her feet.

Isla let herself be led, her body moving on autopilot. Greg's eyes were barely open, his breathing shallow and strained. He whispered something that sounded like a warning, but his voice was too faint to understand.

Clara and Isla both looked towards the window. James was gone.

Then came the first hammering blow to the door.

"Let me in!" James's voice was guttural, a low growl that rumbled through the walls. The wood shuddered beneath the force of his fists, and Isla flinched at each strike. "Let me in, Isla!" he yelled again, his words echoing, making the windows rattle.

Isla felt a chill run down her spine. This wasn't the man she had married. This was someone else, someone darker, more terrifying. She turned to Clara, who was furiously tapping away at her phone, fingers moving so quickly they were a blur.

"What are you doing?" Isla's voice came out breathy, shaky.

"Calling the police," Clara replied, her words clipped and focused. The intensity in her eyes made it clear she wasn't looking for permission or input.

"No," Isla pleaded, shaking her head. "Not yet. Let me try to talk to him first."

Clara hesitated, her eyes narrowing. "You want to talk to him?" she asked, incredulous. "He tried to kill me, Isla. He's out of his mind."

Isla knew it made no sense, but she needed to reach him, to find some sliver of the man she thought she knew, buried beneath this rage. "Just... just give me a chance," she begged, her voice quivering with desperation. "Please, Clara."

Clara's face hardened, lips pressed into a tight line. She looked at her phone, thumb hovering over the screen, and Isla could tell she was weighing her options. After a long, tense moment, Clara sighed, and without a word, she pressed a final button, locking the phone.

"Isla!" James's voice cracked, desperate now. "Open the door! Let me in!"

Isla rested her back against the wall, feeling the vibration from each impact. She took a deep breath, her lungs burning with the effort, and tried to calm her racing heart. She could do this. She had to do this.

She stepped forward, reaching for the door handle, but Clara grabbed her wrist, her grip strong and unyielding. "Don't be stupid," Clara hissed. "You don't know what he's capable of."

Isla met her sister's eyes, seeing the bruises, the fear etched into every line of her face. But beneath that fear was something else—a raw, unwavering determination to protect them both. Isla nodded, acknowledging Clara's warning, but gently pulled her arm free.

"James," Isla called through the door, her voice steady despite the adrenaline coursing through her veins. The pounding stopped, and there was a long, heavy silence. She swallowed hard and took another step closer. "James, please, listen to me."

She could hear his breathing, harsh and ragged, just on the other side. He was so close, but it was as though miles separated them. Isla pressed her forehead against the cool wood, closing her eyes. She tried to picture his face, the way he used to look at her, the way he used to smile.

"Isla," James said, his voice low and almost pleading. "Open the door. We can talk about this. I just want to explain."

Isla felt a glimmer of hope—maybe he was coming back to his senses, maybe he —

Another thud, this time heavier, made her jump. The door creaked under the pressure, and Clara's eyes widened. "He's trying to break it down," Clara whispered, her voice barely audible.

"Let me in!" James roared, his tone turning menacing once more. He began hammering against the door again, each blow stronger than the last. Isla's resolve was wavering, fear gnawing at her insides. How long could the door hold? What would he do if it didn't?

The noise of the door shaking under James's attack was terrible enough, but when it ceased, the silence was even more dreadful. Isla's breath caught in her throat as she strained to listen. Clara's fingers hovered over her phone, her eyes locked on the door, waiting for the next move.

Then they both heard it—a scraping noise outside, something heavy being dragged.

"Oh no," Clara whispered, eyes wide. "What is he—"

Isla had a feeling that whatever James was about to do, it would not end well for any of them.

Before either of them could react, the first strike hit the door.

"The axe," Clara gasped. "He's got the axe."

Isla had been grateful for the neatly chopped logs she had haphazardly thrown on the fire. Even in the chaos of the night, they had given a warm rustic feel. Now, she was seeing the cost.

The blade buried deep into the wood with a sickening thud, splinters flying inward. Clara let out a muffled scream, her hand flying to her mouth. Isla's stomach twisted, panic threatening to choke her. She wanted to run, but her feet were glued to the floor.

Another blow landed, this time deeper. The wood groaned under the pressure. Greg stirred, letting out a pained moan as if the sound of the axe was reaching through his disoriented haze.

Isla's mind flashed back to dinner only hours earlier. James's "Here's Johnny" joke didn't seem so funny anymore. Now, with each strike against the door, it was as though that joke had been a premonition—a dark foreshadowing of the monster he was becoming.

"Can we move him?" Clara whispered urgently, glancing down at Greg. He was trying to sit up, but his eyes were unfocused, and he seemed unable to hold his head steady.

"We have to try," Isla replied, her voice low and tight. They each took an arm, trying to lift Greg, but he was a dead weight, too dazed to support himself.

Another strike hit the door, the axe biting deeper, and the wood began to crack along the frame.

"Can we make it upstairs?" Isla's voice was barely audible over the frantic beating of her heart. "Let's put some space between us and..." She couldn't bring herself to say her husband's name. "Him," she hissed instead.

Clara nodded quickly, glancing toward the staircase.

Isla’s mind raced. It was difficult to come up with a plan when all she could think about was why the hell her husband had turned their Xmas break into an Xmas breakdown. Everything was falling apart in the worst possible way. They had to get to safety, and they had to call the police. Isla realised that now. There was no reasoning with him. They needed backup, and Santa sure wasn’t coming to save them.

“The bathroom in The Pine Room,” Isla said with sudden vision. “We can block the bedroom door and then use your Santa to barricade the bathroom. It’s our best shot.”

“And phone the police?” Clara asked, her voice barely a whisper.

“Yes,” Isla said, her throat dry. “And phone the police.”

CHAPTER TWENTY

Clara nodded.

"Okay. Help me with Greg."

With great effort, they pulled Greg up, each of them struggling to keep him steady. His feet dragged along the floor as they half-carried, half-dragged him toward the stairs. Isla's muscles strained under his weight, every step feeling like an eternity, but the fear of what was coming kept her moving.

"Can you manage your phone in your other hand?" Isla asked. "For the torch. It's pitch black up there."

Clara fumbled in her pocket and retrieved her cell.

"My battery isn't looking good," she said. "But we need to see our way."

"Let's move," Isla said, her voice tense and urgent.

The next strike from James was louder, the axe splintering the door. He was almost through. Clara glanced over her shoulder, eyes wide with terror. They made it to the staircase and started up, Greg groaning in confusion, his head lolling. Clara kept one hand on her phone, shining the beam in front of them.

The wooden stairs creaked under their weight. Each step sounded impossibly loud. When they reached the landing, Isla cast a desperate glance down, back at the door. The hole James had made was large enough for her to see his face, twisted with fury. He met her eyes, and Isla's breath left her. It was like staring into the eyes of a stranger—a stranger who knew exactly where to strike to destroy everything she cared about.

"Go, Isla!" Clara urged, snapping her back to the present. "We need to move him faster."

Isla nodded, trying to steady her breathing, and they rushed toward The Pine Room. Greg's legs nearly gave out, and they struggled to keep him upright. Isla's arms burned, sweat trickling down her back despite the cold, but they couldn't stop now.

The Pine Room loomed ahead, its dark wood giving it a foreboding atmosphere. Isla pushed the door open with her foot, and they manoeuvred Greg inside.

"Let's get him down," Clara said, nodding towards the bathroom door.

Between them, they hauled the semi-conscious man into the bathroom and propped him as comfortably as they could manage against the tub.

"Okay," Isla said. "Let's..."

Before she had time to finish the sentence, the noise of shattering wood came from downstairs.

"Come out, come out, wherever you are," James called maniacally.

He was in the house.

"Help!" Isla yelped in a loud whisper. "Help me move the bed. Block the door."

The two sisters grabbed the bedframe and pulled with all their might. It moved slowly across the carpeted floor.

Too slowly.

"Come on," Isla pressed. "We can do this."

Clara pushed the bed forward with renewed effort. They managed to move it into position behind the closed door. It wasn't much, but it could buy them a few precious moments.

"Now the bathroom," Clara said, her voice breathless.

They both turned to face the small bathroom door, and Isla felt a pang of dread. She glanced through to Greg, who was half-conscious, muttering incoherently.

He wasn't going to be able to help them.

James's footfalls as he climbed the stairs were heavy, each one filled with menace.

"Why is he doing this?" Isla said, turning her pleading face towards her sister.

Clara bit her lip and waved towards the bathroom door. "Not now. Go, go, go!" Clara urged, and they rushed into the bathroom, shoving the heavy Santa in front of the door.

Isla held her breath, listening. The sound of footsteps reached them, slow and deliberate. James was in the upstairs hallway.

Clara's phone was at her ear, her face pale. "It's ringing," she whispered. "I'm calling them."

Isla nodded, sinking to the floor against the cool tiles. Her limbs were like lead, and her head was spinning. She tried to focus on her breathing, to keep herself from falling apart, but all she could hear were James's footsteps, getting closer and closer.

She swiftly pulled out her own phone, turned on the torch, and set it on the edge of the sink to provide at least a little extra light. Then she squeezed her eyes shut, praying the police would answer in time. Praying they'd get here before the last barriers between them were broken.

The call connected, and Clara spoke with brisk urgency.

"What's your emergency?" The voice from Clara's phone sounded tinny and far away.

"He's trying to kill us," Clara gasped into the phone. "My brother-in-law, he has an axe, he's breaking in—"

"Okay, I'm going to need some details." Clara could hear the dispatcher talking to someone away from the phone and then he was back. "What's your location, ma'am?"

"The Morrison retreat. Mountain Pass Road. Please hurry! He's coming. And... and... we need medical assistance. My husband. He's been hurt. He's..."

Clara couldn't keep it together. Isla took the phone.

"Hello? Please. We need police and medical assistance. We're in trouble. Please."

There was a pause that seemed to last forever. "Ma'am, the roads are currently closed due to the storm. We'll dispatch units as soon as—"

"No, you don't understand! He's breaking through the door! And Greg... my brother-in-law... I think he has a... he has a head injury. I don't know how bad it is, but..." Isla's voice gave up on her too, and broke. "We are in danger. We are in *immediate* danger."

Speaking the words made everything too real.

"Barricade yourself in a room with a solid door," the dispatcher said. "Use furniture to block entry points. Stay away from windows. We'll get someone there as soon as we possibly can."

From the bedroom, they heard the thudding of the axe, the cracking of wood. The door hit the bedframe with a dull thwack.

"Greg, is it? Your brother-in-law? Is he conscious?" The dispatcher was taking down notes, asking the right questions, but ultimately, unless someone could get to them soon, it would be for nothing.

"He's breathing. He's unconscious, er, semi-conscious at the moment," Isla said.

"Tell them about his condition," Clara said.

Isla's face fell in confusion. "I don't know," she said. "I don't know anything about him."

James's voice rang out, too close.

"No one's coming to help you," he said, his voice singsongy and terrible. "Not in this storm. Not in time."

Isla looked at Clara, and her sister looked back.

"Is that the perpetrator?" the voice on the line cut in. "Do not engage with him," the dispatcher's voice was firm. "Don't respond to anything he says. Stay quiet, stay together. Try to keep barriers between you and him. If he breaks through, look for anything you can use to defend yourselves, but do not confront him unless you absolutely have to."

"Still on the phone? Still hoping someone will save you? No one's coming. No one can reach us," James repeated. "It's just us now. Just *family*."

Isla's knuckles were white around the phone. The dispatcher was still talking, offering advice they all knew would come too late.

He had an axe, and they had each other.

And outside, the snow continued to fall, silent and relentless, as the nightmare deepened.

The bathroom door shuddered under the first impact as James swung the axe.

The second strike sent splinters flying.

The third broke through.

CHAPTER TWENTY-ONE

Then everything happened too quickly.

The world switched to slow motion.

James burst through the splintered door, axe raised high, his face a mask of rage and triumph. In that frozen moment, Isla saw Greg's eyes focus suddenly, clarity replacing confusion. His leg shot out, catching the heavy Santa model and sending it tumbling into James's path.

James went down hard, the axe clattering against the tiles as his head cracked against the porcelain tub with a sickening thud. The Santa's painted smile seemed to mock him as it lay on its side next to him, the model's eyes directly in line with the man's.

Clara lunged for the axe, but James, even dazed, was faster. His fingers closed around the handle, yanking it away from her grasp.

"No!" she said.

Isla dropped the phone, darting to the far wall, where the Santa had been standing. The Ghost of Christmas Present was going to come in handy after all. As the Santa had toppled, she had seen it: the poker she had stood against the wall earlier in the evening.

Isla didn't think. She moved.

The poker was solid in her hands as she grabbed it.

James was scrabbling to pull himself up, his arm extended to the axe.

Isla brought her foot down hard on his forearm, channelling every ounce of betrayal and fear into the motion. James howled, his fingers spasming open. The axe clattered to the tile once more, and this time Clara was ready. She snatched it up, backing away until she hit the wall, holding it like she wasn't quite sure what to do with it.

Greg managed a small, proud smile from his position by the tub.

"That's my girls," he mumbled, still not fully coherent but aware enough to appreciate the moment.

The dispatcher's voice was still coming from Clara's dropped phone, tinny and urgent: "What's happening? Are you alright? We have units on their way to you."

James laughed, the sound chilling despite his prone position. Blood trickled from where he'd hit his head, staining the pristine white bathmat.

"Don't engage," the dispatcher called out. "Do not—"

The phone lay forgotten on the floor, the dispatcher's voice a constant reminder that help was coming. Clara adjusted her grip on the axe, her eyes never leaving James. "Stay down," she said softly. "Please don't make this worse."

Isla's arms trembled from holding the poker ready, but she didn't lower it. The bathroom was impossibly small with the five of them - four people and one fallen Santa.

"You don't understand," James said, his voice almost gentle now. Reasonable. Like he was explaining something simple to a child. "This was all for us, Isla. For what we deserved. What they took from us..."

"Shut up," Isla whispered. Then louder: "Shut up!"

"Your sister," James continued as if she hadn't spoken, "living off what should have been yours. Pretending to be something she's not, in this borrowed house with her broken husband—"

"I said shut up!" The poker wavered in Isla's grip.

"He's trying to distract us," Clara said sharply. "Don't listen to him."

James's laugh held an edge of hysteria. "Oh, that's rich coming from you, Clara. Queen of deception. Does Isla know why you really invited us here?"

Isla wavered, her eyes turning to Clara.

"I just wanted you to have a good Christmas. No matter what *he* says," Clara said. There was no trace of mistruth in her expression. "I wasn't there for you, when Lillian passed. I did nothing to help. We hadn't spoken for all that time, and..."

"I know," Isla said. "I understand."

James shrieked a high-pitched laugh. "She was my aunt. We spent all of our time, all of our money once hers ran out..."

"And we would do the same thing again," Isla said flatly. "It was never about the money for me. I didn't think it was for you, either."

"Perhaps if we had our own money," James said. There was no concealing the bitterness. "You had money, and you just gave it to Clara. That money was meant to be yours. Your mother left it to you. Do you think she wanted Clara to have it? Don't you think that if your darling mother had wanted this excuse of a woman to have our money, she would have left it to *both* of you?"

Isla took a deep breath. Without stepping off James's arm, she leant towards her sister and put her hand out towards her.

"I *wanted* you to have the money," she said. "We didn't need it. I didn't need it. I had everything, growing up. All of Mum's attention."

"All of her love," Clara muttered. She brought her hand up to her mouth, as if the words had come out involuntarily and she was trying to push them back inside.

"No," Isla said emphatically. "Not all of her love. And I never wanted you to feel that. That was why. That was why I gave it all to you."

Clara's eyes were brimming with tears.

"And she just resented it. She resented you. Resented that you were Mummy's favourite," James was almost laughing.

Isla shook her head. "We should never have let it come between us. Clara was stubborn..."

Clara nodded, just once.

"Proud."

Clara nodded again.

"And I... I was just hurt that I had tried to do the right thing and she still pushed me away."

Clara looked down and wiped her eyes.

"I know," she said.

Isla addressed her sister directly now.

"Before Mum died, she spoke to me. She told me what she had done, cutting you from the will. She said that she didn't think you would spend the money wisely, that you weren't responsible enough. She didn't want you to waste it." Isla raised a hand to silence Clara's defensive interjection before she had a chance to speak.

"I knew she was wrong. I knew you just needed a chance," Isla said, her voice as calm as she could force it to be, given the circumstances. "And I had already been given so much, so many chances of my own."

"We..." James stuttered. "We needed that money. Three hundred thousand pounds, Isla. Three hundred thousand."

Isla looked down at her husband and pressed her foot down more firmly on his arm.

"How did you know? The exact amount – how did you know? I told you what I had done. I didn't tell you how much. I never told you that." Isla could hear the dispatch officer on the line, but all she could do was keep talking to her husband.

"I'm not stupid," he hissed. His voice was leaden with pain. "Get off my arm, Isla. You both have weapons now. I have nothing. Get off and let's talk. Okay?"

Isla looked at Clara. Clara looked at Isla. They both looked at Greg.

Greg shook his head. One firm, decisive movement.

Outside, the storm continued to rage, but it was distant, unreal. Their world had narrowed to this small space, these few moments between violence and resolution.

James shifted slightly, testing Isla's pressure on his arm. She pressed harder, making him grimace.

"This," Isla said, hesitant. "This was all three years ago. Mum. The money. Why now? Why tell me to come here?"

Clara let out a small sigh.

"It was James's idea. This Christmas break for you. He called me a couple of weeks ago. I did that thing where you keep letting the call go to voicemail..." She didn't look proud of the fact. "Eventually I realised he wasn't giving up. I caved and spoke to him."

Isla looked down at James, but he didn't make eye contact.

"He told me about your year. About looking after his aunt. All the time and money you had wasted." Clara made quotation marks with her fingers in the air.

"Wasted?" Isla said. "It wasn't wasted. Without us. Without James. Lillian wouldn't have had even close to the quality of life that we helped her to enjoy during her last few months. James was..." She looked at him again, almost incredulous that the person she was describing was the same one that had nearly killed her sister and brother-in-law. "He was an angel. He was selfless, loving, generous with time and money. I fell more in love with him every day, seeing what a gentle, caring man he was."

James groaned.

"I thought we would get that money back," he said. "She had a three-bedroomed house in Brookland. Investments. Cash in the bank. I thought that when she..."

Isla nodded, bidding him to continue. "When she died, yes."

"When she died, that she would have made provisions for me, for us. That she would be grateful." James let his head fall back against the tub, gently this time, and slumped. His fight appeared to have left him.

"And let me guess," Clara said. "You got nothing?"

"Worse than that," James hissed.

Isla sighed. "We lost money. But it didn't matter. Not really. I knew we had done the right thing. I thought James knew that, too."

"Doing the right thing doesn't pay the bills, though. Does it?" James spat.

"No," Isla said quietly. "But that's not why we did it. That was never why we did it." She looked at her husband, really looked at him, seeing the stranger he'd become. "What happened to you, James? When did money become more important than... than everything?"

The dispatcher's voice cut through the tension: "Units are fifteen minutes out. Keep him talking if you can, but maintain your distance."

James laughed, a hollow sound that echoed off the bathroom tiles. "What happened to me? I spent months watching someone die, Isla. Months of my life, our savings, everything we had. And for what? So your sister could live in luxury while we struggled?"

"Luxury?" Clara's laugh held no humour. "Is that what you think this is? We rented this place. Paid.... well, the figure doesn't matter, but... we did all of this to give you a perfect Christmas because Greg..." She stopped, swallowing hard.

Greg stirred against the tub. "Tell them," he said.

Clara's hands tightened on the axe. "Greg's sick. The tremors, the confusion - it's getting worse. He had an accident, and it started all of... this. We wanted to create a perfect Christmas. Together. As a family."

Isla felt the weight of that confession settle over the room like snow. The Santa decoration lay silent witness, its painted smile now seeming sad rather than mocking.

"I never knew," she whispered.

"How could you?" Clara's voice cracked. "We never talk. Not really. Not about the things that matter. That's why, when James suggested we spend Christmas together... That's why I went all out to make it perfect for you."

Isla managed a tight-lipped smile. "This, er, isn't exactly perfect, is it?"

Clara couldn't quite manage to find the humour.

"I wanted to remember what it was like when we were happy, when things were simple." Clara's eyes were filling with tears again.

"When we still had Mum." Isla moved over to Clara as she spoke, reaching out to her.

"When we still had each other," Clara said.

CHAPTER TWENTY-TWO

In the glow of the two phones, with just enough light to see each other's faces, there was a séance-like quality to the room. The only spirits they were summoning were the ghosts of James's ill-met decisions.

"Why, James?" Isla's voice sounded hollow in the small space. "Why did you have to go so far? Trying to kill them... my sister, Greg..."

James shifted against the tub, careful of Isla's foot still pressed against his arm. In the phone light, blood glistened black against his temple.

"I didn't," he mumbled. "Not at first."

Clara's grip tightened on the axe. "Liar."

"Greg really did fall." James's laugh held no humour. "Genuine accident. Black ice by the generator housing." He turned his face toward Greg. "Isn't that right?"

Greg nodded slowly, his eyes clearer now. "Slipped," he managed. "Hit my head."

"And there he was," James continued, his voice taking on a dreamy quality that made Isla's skin crawl. "Just lying there in the snow. So still. And I thought... well, he's hardly any use anyway, is he? With his condition, his confusion. Whatever's wrong with him. It would be a mercy, really."

"You piece of..." Clara lurched forward, the axe rising. "He's more of a man than you'll ever be!" The words burst from Clara with such force that even the dispatcher fell silent. "His condition...

you do not know what he deals with every day. How strong he is."

Greg's smile was barely visible in the dim light, but it transformed his face.

Clara paused, the axe hovering, and then set it down beside her, as the reality of the situation dawned.

"This isn't me. How has it come to this?" she said, breathless.

"When you volunteered to come out searching with me," James continued calmly, as if there had been no interruption, "it was like a gift. Accidents happen up here in the mountains, don't they? Especially in weather like this. One wrong step near that cliff edge..."

"She's my sister!" The words tore from Isla's throat.

James's eyes found hers in the gloom. "And you're my wife. Everything I did, I did for us. For our future." His voice softened, took on that reasonable tone she'd heard him use with his aunt. "We're drowning in debt, Isla. The care home bills, the medical expenses... I only wanted to talk to them at first. Ask for help. Maybe a loan from all that money you gave them."

"So, you tried to kill them instead?" Isla pressed harder on his arm, making him wince.

"Opportunity," James said simply through his pain. "Sometimes the universe hands you exactly what you need. Greg's fall... it was like a sign. We could have had it all."

One of the phones shifted slightly, sending the Santa's shadow dancing across the wall. The effect was unsettling, as though the séance had gone woefully wrong. Here they all were, summoning ghosts of who they used to be, of the family they might have been.

The dispatcher's voice seemed to come from another world: "Stay calm. Help is coming."

"Tell me exactly what happened," Isla said, her voice barely a whisper. "I need to hear it. All of it."

James shifted, the movement causing Greg to tense visibly. Clara's hand went to the axe, but James just leaned his head back against the tub, closing his eyes.

"I followed him out to the generator," he began. "Watched him try to figure it out. He was... struggling. Confusion setting in. The cold probably didn't help." A small smile played at the corners of his mouth. "Then he slipped. Simple as that. Went down hard on the ice."

The dispatcher's voice cut in: "Sir, we're recording this conversation."

James ignored it, lost in his recollection. "I stood there, watching the snow settle on him. It was beautiful, really. Like one of those Christmas cards where everything's perfectly white. Pure." His eyes opened, finding Isla's in the dim light. "That's when I thought about the money. About how easy it would be. A tragic accident on Christmas Eve."

"But he wasn't dead," Clara spat.

"No." James sighed. "Unfortunately. When he started to move, I... helped him stay down." His laugh was hollow. "But he's stronger than he looks. Managed to get away somehow. Made it back here while I was..." He glanced at Clara.

"While you were trying to kill me?" Clara's voice shook with rage. "Pushing me toward that cliff edge, telling me how sorry you were that it had to be this way?"

The tiny bathroom was even smaller now, cramped with the weight of revelations and betrayal.

"I really did love you, you know," James said to Isla. "Still do. Everything I did was for us. For our future."

"Our future?" Isla pressed her foot harder against his arm. "What kind of future did you think we'd have, built on my sister's death? On Greg's murder?"

"A secure one," James said simply. "No more debt collectors. No more choosing between heating and eating. No more watching our savings disappear into care home fees and medical bills." His voice took on an almost dreamy quality. "We could have had everything we ever wanted."

"Everything... except a... conscience," Greg managed, his words slurring slightly but his meaning clear.

A phone beeped, indicating a low battery. The bathroom dimmed further.

The dispatcher's voice seemed fainter now: "Units are almost there. Keep him talking."

"I watched you," Isla said softly, barely hearing the voice. "You were so good with Lillian." Isla said. Tears tracked down her cheeks. "So patient, so kind. Was any of it real? Or were you just... waiting?"

"All of it," James insisted. "That's what you don't understand. I did it because I loved her. Because it was right. But love doesn't pay bills, Isla. Love doesn't keep the debt collectors away."

The phone lights caught the tears on Clara's cheeks, making them glitter like Christmas tinsel. Greg squeezed her hand, offering what comfort he could from his position against the tub.

"Greg's fall changed everything," James continued, his voice taking on an almost fevered quality. "You were all drinking. I was sober. Who would the authorities believe? Who would you believe, Isla? All it took was one moment of clarity. If he died out there, in an accident... well, Clara would inherit everything, wouldn't she? And then, if Clara had an accident too..." He shrugged. "You'd be next of kin. It would all come to us anyway. The universe providing."

"The universe," Isla repeated numbly. "You mean murder."

"I mean justice," James snapped. "Three hundred thousand pounds, Isla. Three hundred thousand that should have been ours. That could have saved us from all of this."

"You know what's funny?" Clara's voice was quiet but clear. "If you'd just asked, explained about the bills... we would have helped. That's what family does."

James's laugh was bitter. "Family? Is that what we are? It all feels like a lot of playing pretend."

"Better than... playing... murderer," Greg managed, his voice stronger than it had been all night.

The bathroom fell silent except for the storm's constant howl. Through the window, red and blue lights flashed against the falling snow, turning the pristine white into a garish display.

Like Christmas lights gone wrong, Isla thought. *Like everything else about this night*.

James saw them too. His body went rigid under Isla's foot.

"Did you really think you'd get away with it?" she asked softly. "That anyone would believe it was an accident?"

"I thought..." He stopped, seeming to deflate. "I thought it would solve everything."

Outside, the lights grew brighter, turning their little bathroom into a kaleidoscope of colour. Like the Christmas tree downstairs, Isla thought, before everything went dark. Before all their facades cracked and their perfect holiday shattered like dropped ornaments.

The storm was easing, but its damage was already done. Some things, once broken, could never be fixed.

No matter how badly you wanted them to be.

CHAPTER TWENTY-THREE

The bathroom tiles looked like thin ice beneath Isla's feet as red and blue lights strobed through the small window. The colours caught in the fractured edges of the splintered door, transforming James's axe marks into a macabre Christmas light display. Each flash illuminated a different detail: Greg's matted hair, dark with blood; the bruises blooming on Clara's neck; the fallen Santa's painted smile.

"Units approaching structure," the dispatcher's voice crackled, almost forgotten on the floor. "Maintain current positions."

"Police! Coming up!"

Two officers appeared in the doorway, tactical lights cutting through the darkness. Their beams caught the mess of splintered wood, crossed the fallen Santa, illuminated four faces caught in a tableau of betrayal. Behind them, more officers were sweeping the house, their radios crackling with coded messages.

"Subject contained," the first officer spoke into his shoulder mic. His partner moved toward James with practiced efficiency, handcuffs already drawn.

"Sir, I need you to place your hands behind your back."

Isla stepped back, trying to create space.

James complied without resistance, his shoulders slumping as the cuffs clicked shut. The sound echoed in the small room like a full stop at the end of a very long sentence.

"Dispatch," Walsh continued, "we have a male with a head injury, semi-conscious but breathing. Multiple victims. Need medical up here soon as possible."

"Copy," the radio crackled. "Ambulance three minutes out. Be advised we have full audio recording of subject's confession."

James turned his face toward Isla as they helped him to his feet. In the strobing lights, his expression was almost gentle. "At least you're talking to each other now," he said softly. "Family band together in times of crisis. You can thank me for that, at least."

Isla's stomach turned. Even now, he was trying to craft a narrative where he was the noble one, as if confessing to attempted murder after being caught somehow made him generous. As if bringing them together somehow compensated for the pain and betrayal.

"You don't get to do that," she whispered. "You don't get to make this into something beautiful. This isn't a Hallmark movie."

Clara reached out and took hold of Isla's hand.

The officers pulled James to his feet. They flanked him, guiding him towards the splintered doorway. He stumbled slightly on the fallen Santa, and Isla caught a glimpse of his face in the red and blue glow from outside. There was something unfamiliar in his expression – not quite remorse, but a kind of hollow resignation, as if he'd finally realised that some performances can't be sustained forever.

"We need more light in here," the officer radioed to his team. "Medical can't work in these conditions."

"There's a generator," Isla said, the words automatic despite everything. "Behind the house. It needs to be reset after a power cut."

Clara gave her a confused look.

"I read the manual," Isla whispered.

"Copy that," crackled a response. "Heading to check it now."

"Watch your head," one officer warned as they manoeuvred James through the doorway. The warning seemed darkly ironic, given what he'd done to Greg.

James's footsteps faded down the hall, each one punctuated by the gentle jingling of Clara's crystal ornaments, like bitter little bells marking his exit from their lives. A sudden hum filled the house as the generator kicked in, and light flooded up from downstairs. Clara reached out and flicked the bedroom switch, harsh brightness replacing the tactical lights and making everyone squint. In the sudden clarity, the crime scene looked worse somehow – blood red against white tile, splinters forming sharp patterns on the floor.

Despite everything, Isla had an innate urge to follow the officers and the man who was still her husband. Her protective, caring instinct was genuine, unlike James's. She took one step toward the door before Clara's hand found her arm, anchoring her in place. The touch reminded her that some bonds were worth keeping, while others needed to be broken.

When the paramedics arrived, Isla and Clara stepped into the bedroom, creating space in the bathroom for them to work. The two sisters sat on the edge of the bed, just as Isla and James had earlier in the evening. Their view was blocked by the splintered door and the back of the lead paramedic, but they could hear the two uniformed men asking questions, and Greg responding as best he could.

"Sir? Can you tell me where you are?"

"Little place. Mountains," he managed. "Christmas."

"Good. Do you know what happened to your head?"

"James," Greg said, then stronger: "James happened."

Isla had a firm grip on Clara's hand.

Clara squeezed gently.

"I *am* glad he got us back together," she said.

Isla shook her head emphatically. "He's not a hero in this story. Don't make him out to be. What he did was toxic and evil. I'm tired of stories where the villain has a freaking redemption arc. James would have straight up murdered you. Bringing us back together should have been on us, not him."

Clara looked at Isla, considering her words.

"Then I guess you're the hero," she said.

"I'm just a girl sitting next to her sister, wondering how the heck we ended up like this."

Isla reached her arms around Clara and took her into a hug.

Clara winced slightly.

"I might have to get checked out too, I think. There are a few bruises that my adrenaline has let me ignore for a while."

The paramedics loaded Greg onto a stretcher. Clara and Isla followed on behind. The hallway that had seemed so grand earlier was now claustrophobic as they made their way along it. Isla caught glimpses of the Christmas tree below, its lights restored now that someone had properly reset the generator. The ornaments she'd admired just hours ago looked garish, like costume jewellery trying too hard to be real. Her silver star sat on the table, still waiting to be placed.

The room was a chaotic mess. Blood from Greg's head wound had soaked into the expensive throw pillow Isla had used to make him comfortable, turning the cream silk into a Rorschach test of rust-coloured stains. Splinters of oak door lay scattered across the rooms like macabre breadcrumbs, marking James's path of destruction. The pristine carpet – which Clara had proudly shown off just hours ago – now bore the evidence of their nightmare: melted snow tracked in by police boots, and dark patches that might have been blood.

"I'm not sure you're going to get your deposit back on this one," Isla said, her voice flat with exhaustion. She nudged a piece of splintered door with her toe.

"I can't wait to see what their review says," Clara replied with a hollow laugh. "Guests left the house in a bit of a mess. Beware of homicidal tendencies."

They shared a look, hysteria bubbling just beneath the surface. What else could they do? When your perfect Christmas turns into a crime scene, when your husband tries to kill your sister, when everything you thought you knew shatters like expensive ornaments – sometimes gallows humour is all that's left.

Clara cleared her throat, trying to hold herself together.

"I need to go with Greg," she said, her voice rough with exhaustion. "But you should rest, try to—"

"No." Isla surprised herself with the force of her response. "We're not separating. Not now. Not after everything."

Understanding passed between them like a current. All those years of silence, of assumptions and misunderstandings, seemed to crystallise in the frosty Christmas Eve air.

"I never hated you," Isla said quietly. The truth was different now, more raw somehow. "I thought giving you the money would help. Would prove that you mattered. That you weren't second best."

Clara's laugh caught on a sob. "And I've spent three years trying to prove I deserved it. Feeling bad that you gave it to me. Feeling worse that Mum didn't. This whole ridiculous charade..." She gestured at the house with its borrowed luxury. "I just wanted to show you I could be what Mum thought I couldn't."

Stretcher wheels crunched through fresh snow as the paramedics loaded Greg into the ambulance. The sound seemed to punctuate their conversation, marking the end of one chapter and the beginning of another.

CHAPTER TWENTY-FOUR

SIX MONTHS LATER

Steam rose from the pasta sauce simmering on Isla's stove, filling her small apartment kitchen with the scent of basil and garlic. Things had changed a lot in the months since Christmas. Even though she was on her own now, she had made a commitment to herself to continue cooking for herself. There would be no ready meals, no shortcuts. Something about creating food from scratch was healing, like proving to herself that she could nurture and sustain without losing herself in the process. Each chopped herb, each carefully stirred pot, was an act of reclaiming control, of finding beauty in the simple things that James had never appreciated.

Now she was on her own she appreciated the smaller details all the more.

The doorbell chimed at exactly six, right on schedule. Clara and Greg never missed their weekly Wednesday dinner, no matter the weather or their exhaustion after Greg's therapy sessions.

"It's open!" Isla called, stirring the sauce one final time.

Clara's voice echoed down the hallway as she helped Greg with his coat. His movements were steadier now, more controlled, though he still relied on Clara's subtle guidance. The physical therapist said it was remarkable progress for someone less than a year into recovery from a severe head injury.

"Smells amazing," Greg said, the words coming easier than they had even a week ago.

Clara set a bottle of wine on the counter. Isla handed her the wooden spoon.

"Here, taste this," she said. "Too much oregano?"

The easy domesticity still surprised Isla sometimes - how naturally they'd fallen into these shared dinners, this rhythm of sisterhood they'd denied themselves for so long. Her tiny apartment, with its mismatched furniture and slightly crooked pictures, felt more like home than the house she'd shared with James ever had.

"Remember when Mum used to let us help with dinner?" Clara asked, reaching for the wooden spoon. "Well, let you help. I was too little."

"That's not true," Isla said, handing over the spoon. "She let you stir things."

"Only the cold things." Clara tasted the sauce, nodding approval. "She said I was too clumsy for anything hot. Which, fair enough - remember the Great Pudding Disaster of 1999?"

Isla laughed. "I could hardly forget."

"You know," Clara said, her voice softening, "at Christmas, when I kept bringing up old memories... I wasn't trying to make you uncomfortable. I just thought, after the year we'd all had..."

"I know," Isla cut in. "I didn't believe it then - I thought you were being saccharine, showing off your perfect life in your perfect house. I'm sorry I didn't trust that you just wanted us to have a good Christmas."

"We hadn't exactly been on good terms, had we?" Clara set the spoon down, turning to face her sister. "Not since the inheritance."

Greg cleared his throat softly. "I'll give you two a minute —"

"No," both sisters said simultaneously, then shared a small smile.

"You're family," Isla added. "You should hear this too."

Greg nodded, and sat silently, watching on as the women spoke.

Clara leaned against the counter. "I thought you saw me as a charity case," she admitted. "That giving me Mum's money was your way of saying I couldn't manage on my own."

"Clara, no." Isla moved the sauce off the heat. "I just wanted you to have some stability. I had my career, my savings - I didn't need the money. What I needed was my sister."

"And Mum," Clara said softly. "Having Mum would have been good. But..." She sighed and wiped her tears.

Their eyes met, a moment of perfect understanding passing between them.

"Actually," Clara continued, "about the money..." She glanced at Greg, who nodded encouragement. "Greg's new treatment program - it's expensive. Really expensive. The insurance only covers part of it."

"Then I'm glad you have it," Isla said firmly. "The money. That's exactly what it should be used for."

"Even now?" Clara asked. "With all this... moving away from the city, coming to live in this place, near us."

"I wouldn't have it any other way," Isla smiled. "And I just want Greg to have everything he needs."

Greg shifted in his chair. "Getting better," he said clearly. "Getting stronger. For both of you."

Clara's hand found Greg's shoulder in that familiar gesture of support. "The specialists think with the new therapy program, he could be back at work within a year. The brain is remarkable at healing, they say."

"Like sisters," Greg added with a slight smile. "Healing."

Isla felt tears prick at her eyes, but these were different from the ones she had been fighting for the past months. These were cleansing, hopeful.

"I do have one little snippet of news," Isla said. "I've filed for divorce. Final break from the past."

Clara pulled her sister into a tight hug.

"New beginnings," she whispered.

"New family," Greg added, raising his water glass.

"Speaking of James," Clara said carefully. "Or maybe we shouldn't?"

Isla shrugged silently.

"Have you heard anything?" Clara asked.

Isla nodded, draining the pasta with perhaps more force than necessary.

"His lawyer called yesterday. He's agreed to plead guilty. Apparently, he's been attending therapy sessions in custody. Talking about control and money and..." She set the pot down with a clang. "I don't want to know. I don't want his explanations or his excuses or his growth journey."

"You don't have to," Clara said softly. "You don't owe him anything."

Greg cleared his throat. "My words... they don't always come right now. But I see more clearly, sometimes. Since the accident." He looked at Clara, then Isla. "What James did – trying to hurt us for money. It's him that's broken. Not you."

It made sense, in a Greg kind of way.

Isla served the pasta, letting the familiar motions ground her. Her hands shook slightly as she sprinkled fresh basil over each plate. "I keep thinking about his Aunt Lillian," she admitted. "How gentle he was with her. Was any of it real?"

"Maybe that's the scariest part," Clara mused, carrying plates to the table. "Maybe it was real, and the money thing was real too. People can be both – kind and cruel, generous and greedy."

They settled around the table, this little family they were rebuilding from splinters and trust and Wednesday night dinners. Steam rose from their plates like prayers, like promises.

Isla looked around her small kitchen, at the walls she'd painted herself and the slightly wobbly shelf Clara had helped her install last week. At Clara herself, who'd finally stopped trying to prove herself worthy of love. At Greg, finding his words again, one day at a time.

"To family," she said, lifting her glass. "And to real things, even when they're not perfect."

The sunset painted her kitchen walls in shades of gold and rose, turning ordinary moments into something precious. They were healing. They were home.

And sometimes, Isla was learning, that was the greatest gift of all.

CHAPTER TWENTY-FIVE

THE FOLLOWING CHRISTMAS

The front door of the house flew open, and Clara came rushing out, all smiles and wearing what had to be the world's ugliest Christmas sweater – complete with a light-up Rudolf nose and actual jingle bells.

"You're here!" she called, hurrying down the path. "We were about to start the mulled wine without you!"

Clara engulfed Isla in a hug that smelled of someone who had spent the afternoon standing over the oven. Her hair was pulled back in a messy ponytail, flour dusted on her cheek, and she'd never looked more beautiful.

"Oh, Isla," she murmured, squeezing tight. "I'm so glad you're with us. This Christmas is going to be perfect – and I mean actually *perfect*."

Isla followed her sister into the house. The hallway was warm and inviting, filled with the smell of roasting duck from the kitchen. Christmas carols played softly from an old radio that had belonged to their mother.

"This feels pretty perfect already," Isla smiled.

"What, you mean you don't miss the eco-warrior smart house?" Greg called from where he was checking the oven. His movements were fluid and confident, no trace remaining of last year's tremors. "With its million-dollar view and weird photos everywhere?"

"Goodness, who frames their wedding photo and hangs it above their bed anyway?" Clara shuddered dramatically as she reached for the wine glasses – proper wine for her and Greg, sparkling apple juice for Isla, a choice they all respected without comment.

"And that awful Santa in the bathroom," Isla added. "What an eyesore."

Greg and Clara exchanged a glance, their expressions suddenly serious.

"Well," Clara said carefully, "you might not want to go upstairs then..."

Isla's eyes widened in horror before she caught the twinkle in Greg's eye.

"Too soon?" he asked, grinning.

"Way too soon," Isla laughed, picking up a dish towel and throwing it at him. "You two are terrible."

The kitchen timer chimed, and Greg moved to remove the duck from the oven. His hands were rock-steady as he transferred it to the carving board. Clara didn't hover anxiously behind him like she might have a year ago – they'd all learned to trust in healing, in progress, in time.

"You know," Greg said as he picked up the carving knife with practiced ease, "I think duck might become our new tradition. I've gone off goose for some reason."

"Can't imagine why," Clara deadpanned, but she squeezed his shoulder as she passed, that gesture of affection that had become their signature.

"I think that's a good thing," Isla said, suddenly reflective. "I loved our family tradition, but... We can start our own traditions, too."

Clara smiled. "I like that," she said, taking a seat and beckoning Isla over to the table. "No place cards this year," she said.

"Well, with only three of us..." Isla spoke, and the words caught in her throat. "I'm sorry. I didn't know how I was going to find it, you know. Christmas."

Isla watched Greg carve the duck with precision, each slice perfect and even. A year ago, he'd struggled to hold a fork. Now he was back at work part-time, his design skills returning stronger than ever. The small portfolio of renovation projects on his desk proved that some things, broken though they might be, could be rebuilt into something better.

Things had changed. Things were still changing.

"Remember how Mum used to insist on goose?" Clara asked. "Said it wasn't Christmas without one?"

"She'd be proud of this spread," Isla said, eyeing the roast potatoes and braised red cabbage as Greg laid bowls on the table.

"I think," Clara said softly, "she'd be prouder of this." She gestured between the three of them. "Us. Together. Real."

Greg brought the duck over to the table and sat with the sisters.

"Perfect," he said.

Then he raised his glass. "To new Christmas traditions."

"To appreciating what we have," Clara added.

"To family," Isla finished. "And appreciating *each other*. Just the way we are."

"Just the way we are," Greg nodded.

The light fixture above them flickered slightly.

The three of them stopped stock still, glasses raised.

Isla's blood ran cold, but only for a brief moment.

There was no power cut.

There was no darkness.

There was no James.

Outside, snow was falling, but gently this time, without malice or hidden agenda. Just winter doing what winter does.

Later, they pulled crackers across the table, paper crowns tilting at odd angles as they read out terrible jokes. Their gifts to each other were simple, but chosen with care.

When Greg mentioned last year's Christmas Eve, there was no flinching, no darkness clouding their eyes. They could hold those memories now without letting them throw shadows over this new chapter they were writing together. Healing, Isla realised, wasn't about forgetting – it was about learning to wear your scars with grace.

They sat together in Clara and Greg's very real home, where the china didn't match because each piece had its own story, where the silverware was a hodgepodge of car boot sale finds and wedding presents from friends who'd known them before they tried to be perfect. The walls held family photos – real ones this time, slightly blurred and imperfectly framed, but alive with genuine moments. And somewhere upstairs there might have been a certain tacky Santa decoration, placed with exactly the right amount of ironic affection.

Clara's terrible Christmas sweater jingled softly whenever she moved. Isla's contribution to dinner – a slightly lopsided but entirely edible Christmas pudding – waited in the kitchen. None of it was perfect, but it was real.

And that, Isla thought as she watched her sister laugh at Greg's worst cracker joke yet (*What did the Christmas tree say to the bauble? Quit hanging around!*) was exactly how Christmas should be. Not a performance of perfection, but a celebration of survival. Of family. Of love that endures even when the power goes out and the masks fall away.

Perfect, in its own wonderfully imperfect way.

THE END
HAPPY CHRISTMAS

Thank you for choosing to read *Xmas Break.*

I hope you have enjoyed the book. If you liked it, please take a few minutes to leave a review on Goodreads, Amazon, or wherever you recommend books to others. Reviews help authors to find new readers and help readers to discover great books.

If you would like to read more of my books, please visit my website, jerowney.com where you can find links to all of my books.

Best wishes
JE Rowney

Made in United States
Troutdale, OR
12/09/2024